A NEW HOME FOR PABLO

A NEW HOME FOR
PABLO

BY CAROL McAFEE MORGAN

Illustrated by Harvey Weiss

Abelard-Schuman
New York

© Copyright 1955
by
Carol McAfee Morgan

Library of Congress
Catalog Card Number:55-8537

Printed and bound in the
United States of America

Published simultaneously in Canada
by Nelson, Foster & Scott Ltd.

CONTENTS

CHAPTER		PAGE
ONE	The Hurricane	9
TWO	Thursday Draws Near	18
THREE	In the Air	26
FOUR	The New Home	36
FIVE	Bingo	47
SIX	Patrolman Cruz	56
SEVEN	Pablo Beats the Drum	63
EIGHT	A Gift from Anita	74
NINE	Fire Bugs	84
TEN	The Award	93
ELEVEN	Patrolman Cruz Takes a Hand	102
TWELVE	Christmas	111
THIRTEEN	The Picnic	122
FOURTEEN	Graduation	135

For
VALERIE AND HOWARD

CHAPTER ONE

THE HURRICANE

Pablo Torres reached the gate of the Puerto Rican schoolyard and started to run toward home. It was not easy to run with his field drum, but he would not think of leaving it where there might be danger. It was the one treasure he owned.

All the school children seemed to be going in the same direction, shouting as they ran. A big boy yelled in Pablo's ear, "The hurricane is coming! The hurricane is coming!" That was what his ninth-grade teacher had said a few minutes before as she rushed into the room from the principal's office: "The hurricane is coming. We are sending you home at once. Tell your mothers to do what the radio says and to keep calm. You will have two and a half hours to get ready if the storm keeps moving as it is now. Class dismissed."

Pablo could not remember the last storm over

his island. He was three then. But he had heard tales from his grandmother.

For the first time in weeks something was important enough to make him almost forget the big dream, New York City and his father. In less than a week he and his family were to go to live in New York City with Papa. Now he remembered his grandmother had told him that hurricanes can be terrible.

Oh, don't let anything happen, please, he thought as he slowed to a walk, with a sick feeling inside. Being the man of the home since his father had left six months before to get work in New York had been fun. Doña Isabela, his mother, did not know how to write, so all the plans had been left to Pablo. But now he suddenly felt afraid and wished his father were here.

"Pablo! Pablo! Wait for me!" Anita, his seven-year-old sister, was running behind him. He had forgotten her. But he would not tell her so—not Anita, who adored him.

"Look at the water, Pablo. Very angry it is, no?" she panted as she trotted along beside him, her bright blue dress blowing above her knees and her soft black hair already damp with perspiration across her forehead. Pablo liked to hear her talk in English. He nodded with a look to the left. Between houses he saw the Caribbean Sea pounding high over shore rocks, and sensed the explosive boom of each black wave as it rose like a wall into the air. Clouds of dust swept down the road. The children ducked their heads, keeping their mouths

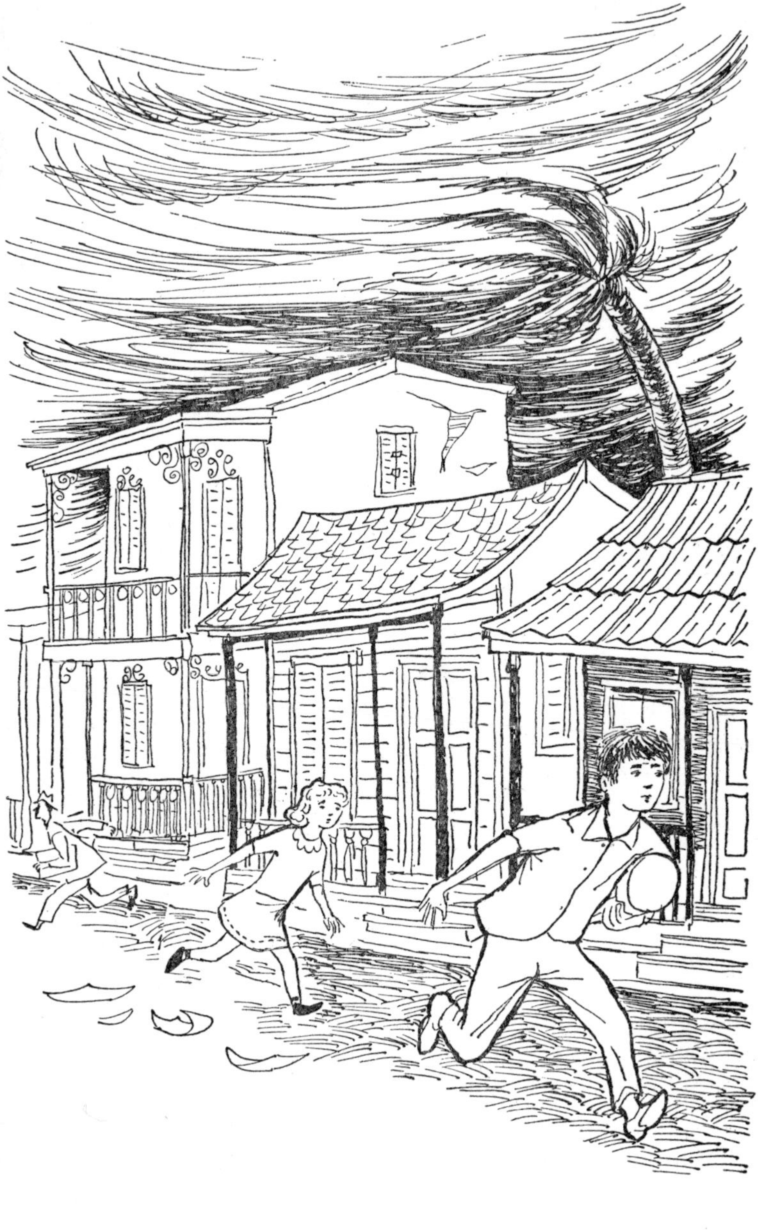

shut and their eyes open only enough to see a little of the street. Pablo's long legs could have carried him much faster, but stocky little Anita must be waited for. Running was not good for her, anyway, for she had a cold.

When they reached their street, Calle Agosto (August Street), with its line of small wooden homes, Pablo was glad to see their mother standing on the sagging porch waiting for them.

"Thank God you are home," she said as she patted each shoulder. "When word came over the radio next door that the hurricane had turned, I knew you'd be sent home. Hurry now, Pablo, to the store. Tomorrow, food may not be found."

Pablo loosened the ropes on his drum, put it carefully into the tin trunk, and fastened the top securely.

"Don't forget candles, son. Without them we may not see when electricity is gone. The blackness is terrible in a hurricane!"

This was said in the gentle voice of the other member of the household, Pablo's grandmother. She had seen many a storm in her seventy-five years and Pablo knew how she dreaded them.

The store was crowded. Customers shouted their wants over the heads of others and all were pushing. The odors of codfish, coffee, gunnysacking, and cheese were familiar to Pablo. Many a day he had helped Don José, his father, in this same grocery store when Don José had been Don Pedro's partner. It was Don Pedro who was to give Pablo the last sixty-five dollars he owed Don José, and it was with this that Pablo would complete payment for their passage to New York.

"My fellow countrymen," the voice of Don Pedro boomed, "in the name of everything, have patience. The storm will not reach us for two hours."

"How you are so smart?" someone called in English.

"The radio, my friend. Had you not been yelling your head off, you would have heard, too." Everyone laughed. "The storm has just passed the east coast. We have two hours, plenty of time to get all you want and for me to get all your money. After that, God take care of everyone."

"Amens" ran across the little store. Then the pushing began again.

Pablo finally had his packages wrapped in newspaper, and rushed toward home. Doña Isabela and Anita were fastening the last wooden shutter of their three-room home with odd pieces of wood nailed from the wall on each side. Grandmother was rocking back and forth in her chair with her worn black Bible in her hands. Reading was difficult now for Grandmother because of her failing eyesight, but she seemed to find comfort in holding her Bible tenderly when she was frightened. She now motioned to Pablo to come closer.

"You're our man, now, son," she said and patted Pablo's arm. "You'll take good care of us all and your papa will be proud of you. Yes, yes, he will be very proud of his Pablito."

Pablo thought of his father waiting for them in New York. How Pablo wished the storm was over!

What was it Miss Thomas at Hanson House had said last Sunday in Sunday School? "If you are afraid, go out and help someone else."

"Mamita," Pablo said, eagerly, "can't we go see how Miss Thomas is? We'll come right back. The wind isn't bad. Please?"

Doña Isabela looked across the street to the neighborhood house. "Yes, you might as well. But come right back," she said.

Pablo took Anita's hand and they rushed across the street. Running past the nursery where they had gone before school days, they reached the patio and the door of Miss Thomas' office. Hammering was everywhere, here as well as on the street, as the handy man fastened doors.

"What are you doing here, my dears? Don't you know a storm is over Puerto Rico?" Miss Thomas asked when they stood in her doorway.

"Yes, we know. But we wanted to see how you are and to remind you that we are going to New York next week," Pablo said in one breath. Miss Thomas sat down abruptly.

"Now just a minute," she laughed. "No one is going anywhere before this storm hits us. It may reach us soon." As she said the last words, the office door blew open, letting in papers and dirt from the street.

"There you are!" she said as she fastened the door again. Then she smiled at Pablo and said in a confidential voice, "I'd suggest that you come over here with your family, Pablo, but I know that would upset your grandmother. Perhaps you had better stay at home. But if your mother is really frightened for your house, you can come here. You know that. Take good care of all your family, Pablo, and tell your mother to give Anita something for that cold. There's lots of sickness now."

The children ran through the swirling dust and were glad to be safely home again. They stood at the door with their mother and watched people running through the streets. Boiling black clouds swooped lower and lower and moved faster and faster overhead.

At last, Doña Isabela drew them through the doorway. "We had better go inside now, my dears," she said quietly. "We'll nail the door." Pablo thought her voice was shaking a little. "Help me here, son. Hold this board tight."

The hammering was soon done. How dark the room was, though it was only four o'clock!

Anita and Pablo felt their way to the little cot

where Pablo slept at nights, and sat on the edge, close together. Doña Isabela pulled a chair beside Grandmother and took her hand. There was nothing to do now but wait!

But the waiting was not long. From far off there came a low rumbling.

"What's that, Mamita?" Anita asked tearfully.

"It's the big wind, dear. But we'll be all right," her mother assured her. Rumbling came steadily closer. Then it hit with all the strength of a demon. It seemed a solid force, like a wall, pushing savagely against the side of the little home. Windows and door shook. A tin pail and pots and pans fell with deafening clatter from the wall and kitchen table. Anita grabbed Pablo's arm and held it tight. Now he felt her body trembling beside him.

Doña Isabela tried to turn on the light bulb hanging at the end of a green cord in the middle of the room. No light! Pablo had heard that when this happened it meant that they were having a real storm. Why was his heart where he wanted to swallow? He got up and went to the shelf and tried to light a candle. No match would flare.

Rain was now falling in torrents. The walls of wind followed each other faster and faster, driving water between the cracks of the wall, around windows, and under the door. Everyone was getting wet. Pablo pulled the cotton bedspread off the bed and wrapped it around his grandmother, who was praying out loud. Anita had run to her mother's lap and he carried two old sweaters to them. Then he wrapped himself in a sheet from his cot and sat up close to the little group, teeth chattering from fright and cold. There were comforting periods of silence when it seemed as if the storm might be over. Then there came the familiar roar and wind again tore at the house. Surely the wooden walls could not stand one more attack but would cave in on them any minute, Pablo thought, helplessly. And if that happened, what of Papa and New York? What would happen to all of them in the end?

CHAPTER TWO

THURSDAY DRAWS NEAR

At the end of two long hours, the storm was over. Doña Isabela found a few pieces of dry clothing to put on each shivering body, wrapping Grandmother in the one dry cotton blanket.

Pablo inspected his drum to be sure it was all right and then he pulled the piece of nailed wood from the door. With a rush, the door opened toward a street littered with debris. Rain was still falling, but the wind was just an ordinary wind now. The children stepped onto the porch. Houses were still standing. People were still living and able to talk. The sound of voices from neighboring porches, inquiring how others were, brought reality back to Pablo.

"Look, Pablo, isn't that Miss Thomas beckoning to us?" Anita asked, pointing to the balcony of Hanson House. For answer, Pablo jumped over the two steps and was on his way. Something told him that Miss Thomas was in trouble.

"Pablo," she called down, "you know where Dr. Perez lives, don't you? Go ask him to come right away. Don Pedro is hurt; Juan just brought him in. Something fell on him in the store. Hurry!"

Pablo heard the last words faintly, for he was already on his way. Jumping over boards, trash, and broken glass, he ran down Calle Agosto through a shortcut to Dr. Perez' home. Fortunately, the doctor was still in.

Pablo's family knew kind old Dr. Perez from the Hanson House Clinic, where he held free consultations twice a week. Everyone loved the doctor. Yes, he would come at once, he said, and getting his bag he joined Pablo. At the door of Hanson House, Pablo left the doctor, feeling sure Miss Thomas would not want him in the way right now. As he drew near Don Pedro's store he could see that the storm had hit the frail building a damaging blow. Carlos, one of Don Pedro's sons, was standing in the doorway looking at the wreckage. There were piles of soaked rice, sugar, red beans that were already swelling with the wetness, coffee, and whatever had been in the glass jars and bottles that now lay smashed on the floor.

Carlos seemed unable to do anything but lean against the wall and shake his head. "Oh, how terrible!" he muttered. "Poor Papa. He was standing here with us looking at the mess when that beam fell on him. We could hardly drag him out. Poor Papa!"

Pablo began thinking seriously of Carlos' poor papa in Hanson House. How badly hurt was he?

A silver coin lying on the floor caught Pablo's eye. As he leaned to pick it up, he remembered. The money! The sixty-five dollars Don Pedro was to give him tomorrow to complete their passage!

"Carlos, what about Don Pedro's money? He had it at home, didn't he?" Pablo asked.

Carlos shook his head. "All that was there in the drawer is gone. Stolen. Over two hundred dollars. The thieves must have come in as soon as the door blew open. They are always ready, those thieves," he said, sadly. It was Pablo's turn to lean against the wall.

"I know," Carlos went on, "you're thinking about the money Papa owes you. But you'll have to wait, Pablo. This wipes him out for now. I don't know how long it will be. We'll pay when we can."

Pablo walked home slowly, stepping carefully

over debris in the street. After they had lived through the hurricane, why did this have to happen?

He explained absentmindedly to Doña Isabela about going for Dr. Perez. Then he sat down on the back step, disconsolately. Grandmother was

watching him closely, he knew. She always knew when he was in trouble. Now she said softly, "What is it, son? What has happened?"

He might as well tell them right now what had happened. There was not much to say. Just a few words and everyone understood. Papa had sent them all the money he could. Everything had depended on that last sixty-five dollars from Don Pedro. And the day for their flight was Thursday of next week, five days off. The little family went to bed very early that night, sadly wondering about their future.

"Pablito, my son, and all of you, look at me," Grandmother said the next morning over their coffee. "I am not much good to anyone now. Leave me here. You have enough money for the three of you. Maybe Miss Thomas will give me a room. I could help her in the nursery, or somewhere else, perhaps."

Leave Grandmother? She had lived with them since Doña Isabela's father died, for as long as Pablo could remember. Anita went to her now and began to cry on her shoulder. Doña Isabela stood with her back to them and rattled pans at the table. Pablo ran his hand through his dark hair and thought he had never felt more miserable in all his life. Then he thought of Miss Thomas. "I'll be back," he said as he jumped off the front porch.

Miss Thomas was in her office. "Thank you for getting Dr. Perez, Pablo," she said as he came in. "Don Pedro has an injured back, but it is not serious." Then she looked at Pablo closely. "I could see from here that your house stood the storm, Pablo. But you seem worried. Sit down."

Pablo sat on the edge of a chair as he told of their problem and of his grandmother's offer. Miss Thomas listened sympathetically.

"Do you want to leave your grandmother, Pablo?" she asked.

"No, of course not. She has always been with us."

"But she is a care, isn't she? Wouldn't you feel more free without her in your new home?"

Pablo's dark eyes flashed as he looked straight at Miss Thomas. His voice rose a little as he said, "We do not think of how much care she is, Miss Thomas. We love Grandmother and she loves us. We couldn't go away and leave her behind."

Miss Thomas' face broke into a broad smile. She opened a desk drawer and pulled out an envelope. "I'm proud of you, Pablo, though I should have known your answer. But maybe there is a way out." She sat looking at the envelope on her desk a moment. "Do you remember the group of North American tourists who visited us for three days last summer at the time you and the other boys were clearing out the old banana patch to make the playground?" Pablo nodded. "Well, the men stood on the balcony and watched you. One of them, a Mr. Patterson, was very impressed by the way you were working. He asked me a lot of questions about you and your family. Then, guess what he did!" Pablo could not imagine.

Miss Thomas lifted the envelope. "He gave me a check for seventy-five dollars and told me to use it for you when and how I wished. I intended to send it to you in New York to help buy winter clothing. But I think you need it right now. What do you think?"

Pablo was speechless. Just because he worked well with his hands, a North American man had left money for him? Funny people, North Americans! And wonderful! Well, he, Pablo, was an American, too.

Miss Thomas handed him the envelope. "Sign

the check, Pablo, after you get to the aviation office, not before. You will want to write Mr. Patterson, so here is his address. Write it in your best English. I told him you are my star English pupil in our night class."

Pablo tried to thank Miss Thomas but it was no use. She understood, he knew.

But when he reached home, Pablo had plenty of words. The good news brought tears and exclamations of gratitude from Mama and Grandmother. Anita jumped off the cot and hugged everyone. Pablo put the check carefully in the tin trunk under his drum, but it stayed there only a few minutes. Why couldn't he and Mamita go to the aviation office this afternoon before it closed and get their tickets? Monday was the deadline, anyway.

With a little persuasion, Mamita agreed, and soon they were on their way. The man at the office took their precious gift check and handed ten dollars back to Pablo. Doña Isabela took the envelope and put it in her straw purse. It was too bulky to go in Pablo's pocket, though he wished he might carry the ticket, just to feel it as he walked along. But Mamita would take good care of it, he knew.

As they passed people on the street, Pablo felt sorry for them. They were not going to New York next week but would still be sleeping here when he and his family were in the plane. And the day they walked into New York City, these people would have nothing to do but still walk these streets and do the things they had always done.

"Wait a moment," Doña Isabela was saying,

laughing as they hurried down the street. "Stop running, son. I can't keep up with you."

As they turned into Calle Agosto, Pablo looked for Anita, but she was not on the porch. When they entered the room they found Grandmother sitting beside Anita on the cot. Anita was sleeping heavily and Grandmother lifted her hand, warning them to be quiet. "She is very hot," Grandmother whispered. "She was crying after you left and then fell asleep. Listen to her breathing. To me, it looks like measles. She seems to be a sick child."

Oh, no! Not measles! Did Grandmother really think Anita had measles? Why, it would take weeks for Anita to get well. They wouldn't be able to go to New York next Thursday.

"I'll get Dr. Perez, Mamita. He is in the clinic now," Pablo called over his shoulder as he rushed out.

CHAPTER THREE

IN THE AIR

Sunday and Monday were anxious days for the little Torres family as they watched beside Anita. Dr. Perez came twice a day and each time examined Anita thoroughly. Each time he said he was not sure. But on Monday night he smiled. "Only a cold, Mrs. Torres. No measles. You can go ahead with your plans."

Now that the danger of measles was over, the Torres family had much to do in the next three days. Most important were the letters and marks they would need for the school in New York. Pablo had expected to get them after school on Friday. The hurricane had changed that plan. So early Tuesday morning he went to their school.

"New York City will be very strange at first, Pablo," the principal said as she handed him the envelope, "but you will get along better than most

Puerto Rican boys because you really speak English. You have Miss Thomas to thank for that, I know. We will miss you here very much, you and Anita. And the drum corps will miss you, too."

Pablo thanked her and shook hands in farewell. How strange it seemed to be walking away from his school, in the middle of the morning, leaving his friends in the classroom. He began to feel lonesome. What if the people in New York couldn't understand him at all? Maybe his English was not so good after all.

When he reached home now, Pablo took his drum from its cloth bag and tightened the ropes. Then he sat on the back step with the drum between his knees and rolled out several simple rhythms. Neighbors were accustomed to this, of course, but he knew they would not understand that he was really playing a good-bye to them. Not a real farewell. That was too final. Just an *hasta la vista*, "until I see you again." Someday he would come back and see this little home and the back yard and Hanson House and the school.

Tuesday and Wednesday seemed to fly, with not enough hours for all that must be done. On Wednesday morning neighbors began coming in and staying for little cups of sweet black coffee and prolonged farewells. Anita grew stronger rapidly. Pablo said silly things to make her laugh. Even Grandmother was caught up in the excitement as she packed her large suitcase and gave Doña Isabela advice on what to put into the cardboard cartons.

The weather was kind. Thursday morning broke

over the island clear and sunny and the Torres family was up at dawn. The house must be cleaned and left in order for the landlord, who was buying the few pieces of furniture they owned. By two-thirty the suitcases and cartons and Pablo's drum were on the porch to show the taxi-driver where to pick up his passengers.

Miss Thomas had invited them to Hanson House for an early supper but only Grandmother was able to enjoy the rice and red beans and fried green bananas. The others were much too excited to eat. Miss Thomas understood and fixed a big bag of sandwiches and oranges for them to take along.

"Here is a note to Ferris Center, near your new home, Pablo," she said after supper. "You will find many of the same things there that we have here, and Mr. Everett will be glad to help you. Take good care of the family until you reach your father and don't let Anita get sick again."

At last there came the sound of a three-toned horn. Miss Thomas and Dr. Perez stood on the sidewalk with a host of neighbors and waved them off.

"Good-bye! Good-bye! Go with God!" came from all around them as the car drove away. Grandmother nodded. "Yes, may we go with God, always."

Anita sat on the edge of the back seat for fear she would miss something. Doña Isabela cried softly in her corner until they were outside the town. Then she dried her eyes and joined the others in watching everything they passed.

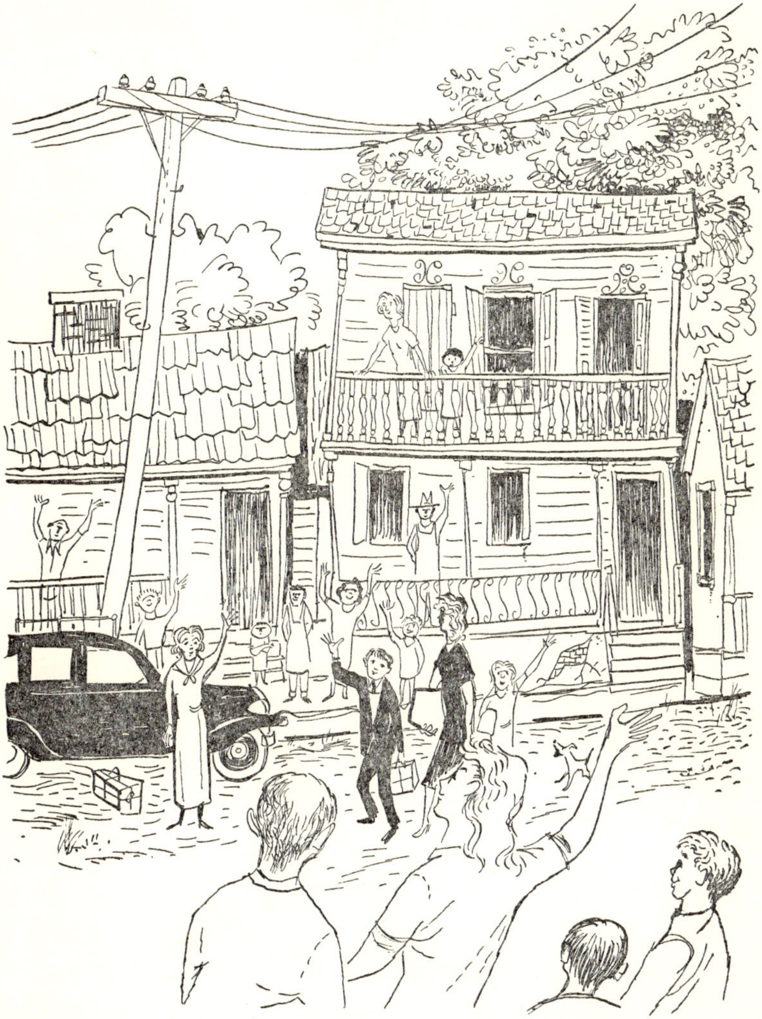

Their road led north between cane fields and then up a steep hill to the bluff where they looked down on the deep blue of the sea.

"We'll see the ocean in New York, won't we, Pablo?" Anita asked. Pablo nodded. No use to tell her that they would not be just a couple of blocks from the ocean the way they were here. But he was truthful; New York was surrounded by water!

Now they were going through a coconut grove along the shore, where shafts of sunlight, between closely growing trees, lighted piles of coconut husks and brown fronds that had blown from the trees during the storm.

Now the taxi was speeding down the smooth military highway toward San Juan. They passed through several north shore towns. Once they stopped to buy cashew fruit. Very carefully they picked off each nut from the blossom end and threw it away for fear the acid inside the green skin would burn their lips. Then they ate the puckery fruit with gusto.

"We won't find these in New York," Pablo said, "nor sugar cane." And he handed Anita a stock of cane to chew on.

"But apples, Pablo, there will be, no?"

"Yes, lots of apples will be there," he answered, laughing. He too preferred apples, but at ten cents each he had not had many.

The narrow streets of San Juan reminded Pablo of their home town, only there were more cars and more horns and more people and more everything. He was glad when they turned into a wide road beside the bay. "Isla Grande" he saw on a signboard.

The kindly driver helped Pablo carry the luggage to the counter inside the big airport building. "I know where to take you, for many times I come here," he had said when they parked the car. Pablo was grateful to him.

"First, you show the man here your tickets," he instructed.

Tickets! Pablo turned to Doña Isabela. Nervously she opened her flat leather bag. With a trembling hand she lifted out a coin purse, some bills, keys, and a handkerchief.

"Mamita, the tickets! Where are they?" Pablo whispered. His mother looked again. Then Pablo took the bag from her, but he did not find them.

Grandmother was watching from the bench. "What is wrong, daughter?" she asked.

"We have lost the tickets," Doña Isabela answered, almost in tears, "but I took them myself at the office of aviation. Where can they be?"

Anita was holding to Pablo's arm, tightly.

Grandmother took the leather bag. "It seems to me..." They could see she was trying to remember something. "It seems to me that you carried your straw bag last Saturday when you went to town, daughter. Think, wasn't it your white straw bag?"

"Oh, what a thing!" Doña Isabela answered in great relief, and knelt to open her suitcase. On top lay the straw bag with the ticket envelope. Pablo, greatly relieved also, echoed his mother's words in his thoughts. What a thing, indeed. No more like that. He'd take charge from here on to New York.

Luggage was quickly weighed and taken away. Pablo put the checks in his own pocket and joined Anita at the gift counter. They walked round the circular counter several times, looking at the dolls from many countries, straw bags and baskets, bead jewelry, wooden articles, post cards and candy.

"I'm hungry," Anita announced as they rejoined Mamita and Grandmother on the cushioned bench. Pablo peeled oranges for each one with his pocket knife and made a deep hole in the stem end so the juice could be squeezed out. Then they settled down to the sandwiches Miss Thomas had given them.

As time went by, more and more people came into the building. One flight to Caracas had just left. With supper over, the family watched other passengers and listened closely for their flight to be called.

At exactly ten-fifteen a voice came over the loudspeaker, "Flight five two eight, gate number one. All passengers for flight five two eight will please go to gate—" The family had already started toward the gate. Pablo had a great sense of release. This was it! Their flight at last. He led the way, carrying his drum, with Anita holding tightly to his other hand. The man at the gate asked the name and looked down the list. "Okay, Torres, four of you, pass on through," he said.

Now they were in the open, walking toward a tremendous airplane. Up the stairs they climbed, single file. At the door a steward and stewardess, both in blue uniforms, welcomed them and the steward suggested that they find seats up front. The stewardess took the drum from Pablo and put it back of the last seat. "It will be all right here and you can get it as you go out tomorrow morning," she said, smiling.

"Here are two seats. Good!" Doña Isabela exclaimed. "You sit with Pablo, Anita, and I will be here across from you with Grandmother."

All around them rose a sea of voices, mostly in Spanish, although there was some English. Hats were put on the shelf overhead and small pillows were pulled from the same shelf. Some were experimenting with their seat backs, adjusting.

"Let me sit next to the window, Pablo. I am smaller than you," Anita begged.

"All right, for now," Pablo answered.

At last the back door was being closed. A red sign lighted up in the front of the plane. "*Abroche su cinturón*," one line said, and under it the same in English, "Fasten your belts."

The steward was coming down the aisle. "May I have your attention, please," he said, facing the passengers. "This is flight number five two eight for New York City. We leave at ten-thirty and arrive in New York City at five-thirty tomorrow morning. Please fasten seat belts. No smoking."

As he passed, he stopped to help Pablo fasten his belt, which he had been sitting on, and Pablo helped Anita. Now the engines were throbbing, first on one side, and then on both. Smoothly the plane moved forward and lights were passing the window. At the end of the runway the plane turned, and after a few minutes of waiting, again moved forward with a great roar of the engines, faster and faster until there was no longer the feel of wheels underneath and Pablo knew that they were in the air. Past Anita he could see the lights of the harbor on the left as the plane dipped and turned. Then it righted itself and soon they were passing through thin layers of clouds that glided past the window, showing up in the light through the window.

But before long, they came out into silver moonlight, above the layers of clouds. Gradually, talking subsided. Lights on the plane were turned off, except where an occasional person was reading by a little light which beamed on his paper from overhead. Pablo looked across at his mother and grandmother. Their eyes were closed. How quickly everyone was going to sleep. A baby that had been crying near the back was quiet now.

Suddenly, Pablo realized that Anita had been very quiet. She was sound asleep. Looking up at the sign, he found that it was off. So he carefully unfastened his seat belt and then Anita's. Gently, he pushed his sleeping sister into his seat and settled himself comfortably by the window. Let the rest sleep, he thought; he would stay awake. He pressed his face to the glass of the window and looked down. For a few minutes the clouds below cleared away and he thought he could see the lights of a ship on the inky water floor. Then they were into clouds that stood upright, like pillars, with wells of moonlight between. Pablo imagined they were mountains and the plane was flying down valleys and around peaks. This was exciting, for a while. But before long, his head settled back.

The next thing Pablo knew, a voice was saying, "We will be in New York City in half an hour."

Still half asleep, he shook Anita. Mamita and Grandmother were already patting their hair and smiling across at him. Daylight was beginning to light the clouds below and some were already rimmed in red. The steward brought the passengers cups of steaming coffee and a sweet roll and there was milk for Anita.

"We changed seats, all right, I guess," Anita laughed, leaning over to look out the window.

"There's land," Pablo said, pointing down, "and there is a city. Look at the cars, Anita, creeping along. They look like ants, don't they?"

"Fasten seat belts, please. We are arriving in New York," the steward was now saying, and the children needed no help this time.

CHAPTER FOUR

THE NEW HOME

Landing was bumpy and Anita put her hands over her ears and made a face. Pablo's ears were hurting, too, as if something were pressing in on them. He was thankful when the wheels touched ground. Now he knew they were really in the United States! Seat belts were unfastened and people began reaching overhead for parcels and hats. A big stairway like the one in San Juan was being wheeled toward the plane and soon the back door opened and passengers began to leave the plane.

Pablo collected his drum on the way out and wondered if anything could have happened to it. But it felt all right through the denim bag.

"This way, please. Collect your baggage inside," a man called. As the crowd entered the Idlewild building there was much calling, embracing, and laughter as relatives and friends met. "I wish Papa were here, don't you?" Anita was walking beside Pablo.

"We will find him after an automobile ride," Pablo answered her, "at some place they call a terminal."

"Go to the right for your luggage," a man in uniform was saying. At a low counter at the end of the building, Pablo handed over their baggage checks to another uniformed man and received their luggage. To get it all out to the waiting automobile was quite a tussle, but the four of them managed, and they were finally seated inside the big automobile with other passengers. A man came inside collecting fares and, from the Torres family, asked for four dollars and forty-five cents. That seemed like a lot of money to Pablo. But they had to reach Papa.

Soon the auto was rolling down the highway, first passing flat wasteland and then homes. Anita kept her hand on Pablo's arm and he knew she was scared. It did seem as if everyone were in an awful hurry. He wondered how the driver could keep his head and keep them on the road with so many other cars whizzing past on both sides. They rolled over several bridges and then down narrow, rough streets with tall houses on each side.

At last they pulled up a street and stopped. "This is your terminal," the driver announced as he pulled the lever that opened the door.

"There's Papa!" Anita and Pablo cried at the same time, waving wildly to the tall, slender man in the dark suit who was standing on the sidewalk.

The children were out the door in a flash and into their father's outstretched arms. How handsome Papa is, Pablo thought, as he stood back while his mother and grandmother were greeted. Papa was heavier and looked as if he felt better than when he had worked in the grocery store.

"So you brought your drum, son." Papa laughed. "You still like your drum, no?" Pablo grinned as he swung the drum bag onto his back and picked up a suitcase.

"Now to the subway, and then we will soon be home," Papa said. When they got out onto the wide street, Pablo stood still and gazed up at the buildings towering high into the sky. It was more magnificent than he had ever dreamed. Anita looked up quickly and then ducked her head and looked at her feet. "I'm scared. What keeps them from falling over?" she asked in a small voice.

"Come on, we are in people's way standing here. Now, follow me," Don José said, and led them down the street, around a corner and then down steep steps to the subway. "Stay right with me, everybody," he called over his shoulder. "I don't want to lose any of my family now."

Papa bought funny little metal pieces at a window. These he put in the slot beside the turnstile as each one pushed the big wooden wheel that turned heavily and let them pass through. All together again, they waited in the damp coolness on the underground platform.

"You must hurry when the train comes. It is in a great hurry and will not wait," Papa said, just as a long train rumbled to a stop in front of them. "Stay close, now," he warned, as a crowd of people, all in a hurry, poured around them from many train doors. At last the family was in the train and there was room for their baggage on the floor at their feet.

"Why did so many get off the train?" asked Anita.

"This is rush hour for some workmen and they all come at once. We will go fast. You will see."

Past lighted stations they flashed, so fast Pablo could not read a single thing that was written on signs, around curves that made him dig his heels into the floor to keep from falling into the aisle. There was no use trying to talk. It was too noisy. "Next stop is ours," Papa warned, "and we must hurry." Is all New York in a hurry, Pablo wondered, and why was everyone having to rush so?

The clear air at the top of the stairway felt

good, though much warmer than the damp air in the subway.

"Three blocks now and we are home," Papa said, as he and Pablo walked together ahead of the rest. "Only it will not be like our home in Puerto Rico, Pablo. You know that, don't you, son?"

Of course Pablo knew it. Why, everything was nicer in the United States!

His father went on. "It is the best I can get now. Someday we will have better. You will see."

Just then three children shouting Spanish passed them on the run. Pablo felt suddenly happy.

"Yes, lots of Puerto Ricans live around here," Papa said, seeing Pablo's smile. Pablo thought it might not be so strange to live in New York, after all.

The narrow street with its three- and four-story buildings rising directly from the sidewalk certainly was not Calle Agosto. The early heat from the pavement where the sun was drying the dampness of the night struck him in the face. There was no sea breeze here. Gray smoke hung in the air and a strange odor filled Pablo's nostrils. They walked past tall iron fences that shut off stairways to basements. "Do people live down there, Papa?" Anita asked.

"Yes, daughter, they live everywhere in New York, anywhere they can find. Sometimes many families live together in one apartment. We are fortunate; we have three rooms for ourselves. Here we are, my dears. This is your new home! It is up three flights." Papa set down his baggage and

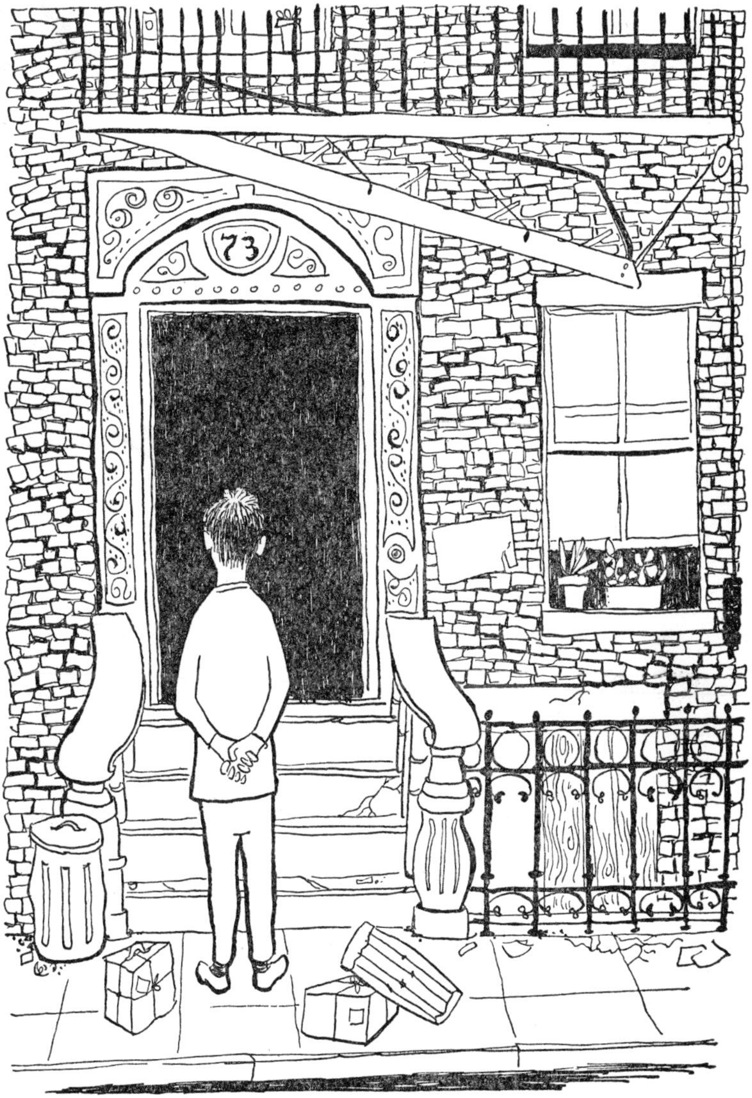
73

hunted for a key. The little family stood around him, nearly filling the sidewalk with their luggage and themselves. Pablo looked up the side of the dirty red brick building that was their new home. What was that funny stairway coming down the front of all the houses in the block?

"A fire escape, son," Papa answered when Pablo asked. "Every house must have one. It is the law, for New York has many fires."

"But it does not reach the street."

"If you were on it, that flat ladder would swing down to the street. It is made that way so burglars cannot get into apartments. Now, up the stairs we go."

Pablo did not like the idea of the stairs in front, but he followed his father, with Anita at his heels. The hallway was dark and smelly and papers lay on the floor. As they passed one closed door they heard someone speaking English. Then through another door came Spanish and through still another door, a language that was strange to Pablo. "What are they speaking in there?"

"That's Italian. We have many languages and many kinds of people in this part of the city. You will see."

They had reached the third floor while Mama and Grandmother were still far below, coming up slowly. Papa was trying to find the hole for his key in the darkness of the hall when a door burst open on the floor above and a scolding voice followed a tall, black-haired boy who was running down the stairs two at a time.

THE NEW HOME 43

"Aw, do it yourself, Josy, and shut up! I'm late for school now," the boy yelled back angrily, nearly knocking Pablo over as he swung around the iron stair post. A girl's high voice came from above again, "All right, Bingo, you'll see when you get home tonight." And she slammed the door.

By this time the boy was looking Pablo over. "You gonna live here?" he asked rudely, pointing with his thumb to the door.

"Si—yes." Pablo suddenly remembered to speak English.

"Oh, moider! Some more spics," the boy exclaimed more rudely than before and raced on down the stairs, all but upsetting the two women on the floor below.

"What does 'spic' mean?" Pablo asked. But at that moment his father opened the door. The children followed Don José into the narrow hallway of their new home. From the hall they went into the kitchen with its little stove and table, and back of this was a little parlor. Pablo went to the window and looked out. All he saw was the wall of the next house a few feet away. Don José pulled the cord on a light that hung in the middle of the room. Though there was sunlight outside, none of it was reaching the blackened windows of their new home. The children went on into the back bedroom and again looked out the window. Below was a cluttered areaway where neighborhood washings were hanging from lines strung between windows and back fire escapes.

Don José stood by, watching his family inspect

their new home. Pablo knew that he was not happy. "Someday, we will have better. You will see," he had said out there on the sidewalk. We certainly will, Pablo thought. Some way, I'll help Papito to get something better someday. But for right now, this was home and they were all together. That was what mattered most.

Grandmother sat down, exhausted, on the faded sofa. Doña Isabela returned quickly from her inspection and opened her suitcase and got out the pound of powdered Puerto Rican coffee. "We will all feel better after some coffee," she said and Pablo knew she was trying not to show disappointment.

Don José put a small teakettle of water on the

stove. "Look here, children, see how we make a fire, so quick." They stood in front of the little three-burner stove. Don José lit a match, turned a knob, and a blue fire came through small holes and kept burning. "It is gas. Much better than charcoal, no?" he asked, putting his arm around Mamita, who smiled up at him. "And here is the refrigerator. I put some things in it. See?" He opened the door with pride and showed them the ice cubes. The children had seen a refrigerator at Hanson House but they had never had one on Calle Agosto. Once in a while they had bought a piece of ice for a drink of lime or bitter orange juice when guests came in. Having such a stove and refrigerator now was wonderful. It must cost Papa a lot of money.

"Everything here belongs to our landlord," Papa explained. "I pay much rent for it, but we will get along. You'll see. And now, I must go back to the hotel. The boss said to be back by ten. There are rice and beans and all you need for today, Isabelita," he said as he kissed his wife good-bye. "I'll be home late tonight. Be sure your door is always locked."

As he went out he motioned to Pablo to go with him. He called back from the door, "I forgot to get lard. Pablo can come with me and bring it back from the grocery store."

Once in the street, Papito put his hand on Pablo's shoulder. "Son," he began, sounding very serious, "you asked what a 'spic' is. That is a word that is used in an unkind way for Puerto Ricans here. If someone calls you that, he means he does not like you. But try to remember that that is just because he has not had a chance to really know you. Act as if you do not hear it and go on about your business. You will make people like you, son. You will see." The words brought comfort to Pablo. Things would not always have to stay the same. His father was talking again.

"When I began working at the hotel, some of the other porters called me names, but they don't any more. You'll make friends. Just be patient, son," and he drew the boy close to him as they went into the grocery store. It was a small store, about the size of Don Pedro's, but much cleaner.

With the pound of lard in his hand, Pablo left his father and went back quickly to the apartment. Why would anyone not like Puerto Ricans? They were citizens of the United States, weren't they? And why, Pablo kept wondering, why didn't that boy upstairs like him?

CHAPTER FIVE

BINGO

The Torres family did not sleep well their first night in the big city. Don José and Doña Isabela had the one bedroom, while Anita slept with her grandmother on the opened-out parlor couch and Pablo bedded down on the hall cot. How strange were the sounds of the city all around, as if a big mixer were jumbling all the noises together and letting them out as one low, continuous roar. Pablo lay listening to it for a long time. What would he be hearing now in their home on Calle Agosto? There would be an occasional auto horn, or a radio, and the booming of the sea. But he would not let himself remember these sounds. Tomorrow would be Saturday and Papa's day off from work. He was going to take the children to see Ferris Center and meet Miss Thomas's friends. Pablo would make himself think about these things. He'd make—

"Pablo, time to get up!" Pablo opened his eyes to find his father leaning over him. "Get up, son. We're going to see things today."

Anita was already dressed and helping Grandmother. Doña Isabela dished up the oatmeal, and a delicious cinnamon odor came from the steaming dishes. Each coffee cup had a few spoons of ink-black coffee essence in it, and when the family sat down, Doña Isabela filled the cups with boiling milk.

"Mmm, just like home," Don José exclaimed. "How I have missed real coffee with milk, Isabelita, and your good cooking. I have missed all of you, more than I can tell you. I hope you will be happy here—"

"Of course we will, son," Grandmother hurried to say. "Of course we are content wherever you are. Now let me ask the blessing."

Pablo liked to hear Grandmother pray. This morning she asked for a blessing on all the family and she thanked God for everything. She always seemed to know God in such a friendly way. What if they had left her behind, Pablo thought again, and he said a silent prayer of his own, a prayer of gratitude for the way things had turned out, and for Mr. Patterson, too. The night before, Papa had been told all about the storm and Don Pedro and Mr. Patterson and had been glad with them that a kind stranger had helped out when they needed it most.

"When can we go to Ferris Center, Papito?" Pablo asked after breakfast.

"At ten o'clock. Mr. Everett will be there by then," Don José answered.

"Then may I take a walk around the block now?" Pablo asked, feeling very independent and anxious to show how well he could take care of himself.

"I guess so, but be back in an hour or sooner," his father answered.

The air felt good as Pablo ran down the outside steps onto the street. He turned to the right and was soon on a street called First Avenue, according to the small sign on the corner.

What a sight the avenue was to Pablo! He had never seen anything quite like it. Row after row of fruits and vegetables along the sidewalk in various-sized piles, on tables, and in boxes and baskets. Pablo was used to outdoor markets, but to nothing so beautiful as this. It looked as if the little shops had burst their front walls and run over into the street, only everything was very orderly. Men in white aprons were polishing apples and straightening piles, or adding fresh things to their supplies, commenting on the excellence of their wares to any passer-by who stopped. Then there were fish markets and tubs of live fish and prepared fish ready to cook, neatly piled in rows. The odor made Pablo think of the waterfront at home.

Just then Pablo thought he recognized a figure ahead. Was that Bingo sauntering along with two other boys about the same size? The three boys suddenly stopped and looked back. Pablo was sure now. Apparently Bingo did not see him. They were walking on, very slowly, past a fruit store. As Pablo

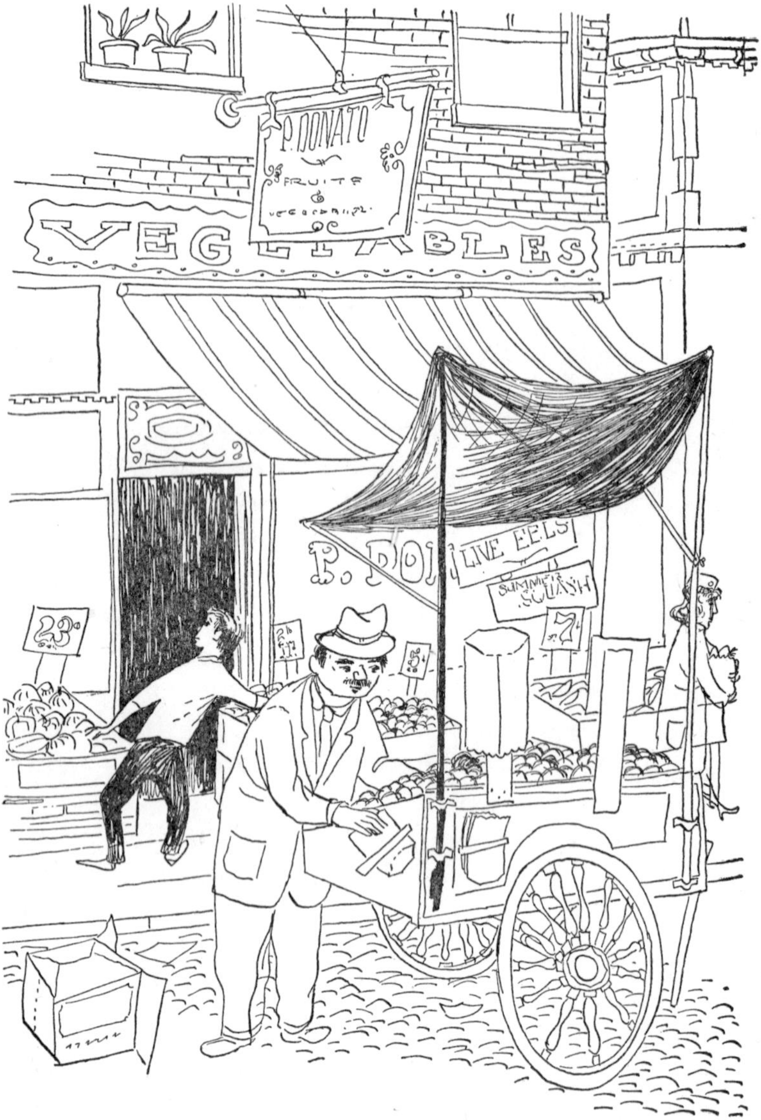
P. DONATO
FRUITS
LIVE EELS
SUMMER SQUASH

came near, he heard one of the boys say, "Go ahead, Bingo. Right now!" Pablo saw Bingo grab several apples from the nearest pile and stick them in his shirt front. The other two had broken into a run and Bingo followed.

So Bingo was mean enough to steal! Pablo looked into the fruit shop, but apparently no one had seen the thieving. His companions were evidently watchers who told him when it was safe. Wouldn't police catch him? Pablo wondered.

A few stores further on, Pablo was startled to find Bingo walking slowly back toward him, hands in pockets. The other two had disappeared. Bingo did not see Pablo, or perhaps he did not recognize him. Well, Pablo would not care to remind him with a greeting. That was sure.

But as Bingo reached Pablo he suddenly pulled two big apples from his pockets and pushed them into Pablo's hands. "Here you are, spic. Have an apple. See how easy it is? A cinch. Let me know any time you want anything. Be seein' you," and Bingo swaggered on down the street, whistling. Pablo stood stock-still. These apples were not his; they were stolen! They belonged back there on the fruit stand.

Pablo looked back to see how far Bingo had gone. When he saw that Bingo was well past the fruit stand, Pablo turned and hurried to the pile of apples. As he got there, the storekeeper went inside and out of sight. Swiftly, Pablo put the apples on the pile and walked quickly toward home, wishing he could break and run. But Bingo was ahead and he certainly did not want to pass him.

Pablo felt very unhappy to see Bingo turn into their apartment house. He slowed his pace to give Bingo time to reach his fourth-floor home before going into the building himself. But luck was against Pablo. Bingo was waiting at the foot of the stairs.

"Easy, isn't it, spic? Why didn't yuh keep 'em, yuh sap?" Bingo asked with a sneer.

Pablo did not know what to say, so he tried to pass Bingo and get on home. Bingo blocked his way. "Scared? I'll give yuh another chance some day. I'll show yuh how to ride the subway. That's easy, too. When are yuh goin' to school?"

Pablo told him that he and Anita would be going for the first time on Monday.

"What grade?" Bingo asked.

"Ninth, I hope," Pablo answered.

"Aw, you're just a kid. I'm in tenth. Be seein' yuh," and he jumped up the stairs three at a time and banged the apartment door behind him.

Pablo found Don José and Anita ready to go to Ferris Center. He would not tell anyone what had happened, at least not now.

The walk to the community house took them ten minutes. Then Don José, with the children following, went through a big glass door into the hall. Here Don José pushed a wall button and something buzzed inside. Suddenly a door in front of them slid open and there stood a man in a big cage. Papito saw the wondering expression on Pablo's face, and he laughed. "Come on. This is an elevator that will take us upstairs," he said. Then he explained to the smiling man, "Their first time in an elevator," and the other nodded. With a bang, the door closed and Pablo felt the whole room around him rising from the floor. When the cage stopped, the man said, "Fourth floor, Mr. Everett's office," and the door opened again. The children nearly tripped each other getting out in a hurry.

"They remember the subway rush, I guess," Papa explained to the laughing elevator man. The ride had been fun. Pablo wished he could ride up and down on the elevator all day.

As the trio entered his office, Mr. Everett rose from behind his desk and held out a welcoming hand. "Well, well, if it isn't the Torres family. How wonderful that you now have your family together, Don José. You must be a happy man right now."

"I am indeed very happy," Papito answered.

The two men talked a few minutes about Don José's work and the hotel and Pablo understood that Mr. Everett had helped his father get the work in the first place.

"And you, Pablo, do you want work too? I am sure we can help you get a paper route after school."

How very kind he is, Pablo thought. Of course he wanted work, and arrangements were made for him to make application for a paper route. Then Pablo remembered Miss Thomas's note. He pulled it from his pocket and handed it to Mr. Everett.

"So my old friend Miss Thomas has written me. Excuse me, please," he said and opened the letter. In a few seconds he looked up, smiling. "Well, young fellow, Miss Thomas gives you a very fine recommendation. I hope she told you as nice things about us here so you will want to be with us a lot. Tell me about Hanson House. How is Miss Thomas?"

Pablo felt the warm kindness of Mr. Everett as he told him about the storm and Hanson House and Miss Thomas and then he told about the trip on the plane.

"Your father is studying English with us two nights a week and is doing very well. But I'm afraid his son is already far beyond him in English. You speak very well, Pablo. No doubt Miss Thomas again?"

Pablo nodded.

"My wife and maybe her mother will come to your first class, Mr. Everett," Don José said. "They do not know any English and that is not good in this land. We Puerto Ricans cannot thank you enough for what you are doing for us. You are very kind, always."

"We try to be, Mr. Torres. That is what we are here for. Remember to come to us any time you need help."

"Yes. And Pablo, you remember that, too," Papito said earnestly. But Pablo did not need to be reminded. He knew Mr. Everett and his associates were his friends, just as Miss Thomas was.

There was a knock at the office door and a policeman entered. Mr. Everett greeted him cordially. "Ah, Patrolman Cruz. Here are two of your countrymen, Pablo and Anita. They just came from your island yesterday. You know their father, I think." The two men exchanged smiles and shook hands.

"So, you are really new here, Pablo," the policeman said, smiling. "I hope you like basketball. Join us here in the gym next Friday night when PAL has a practice for your age group. We'll be glad to see you." After speaking further with Mr. Everett about a family on his beat who needed help, the policeman left.

"What does PAL mean?" Pablo asked.

"That is a group run by policemen for the boys and girls of the community," Mr. Everett explained. "The letters stand for Police Athletic League. They have all kinds of athletics for you boys and they use our equipment here. And Anita," he added, turning to her, "we have a club for you, too, where you can learn to make all kinds of things, even doll clothes. Would you like that?"

Of course she would!

After getting the days and hours for club meetings, and promising to be in Sunday church-school tomorrow morning, the family left for home.

In the narrow street children were everywhere, pitching ball until cars or trucks honked them off the street. Little girls chased each other up and down steps and over iron fences, while older young people stood in doorways, talking and laughing. Pablo saw a group of Chinese, like Mr. Lee who ran the restaurant near Calle Agosto, ironing clothes inside a big glass window. All around, strange languages were being spoken. He wondered if he would see some of these boys on Monday at school. Somehow, he dreaded Monday when he must go to school. But he must not show the family how he felt. He was no coward. Yet he did hope Bingo's room at school would not be near his.

CHAPTER SIX

PATROLMAN CRUZ

The next day the Torres family dressed in their best to go to Ferris Center, all but Grandmother, who insisted that she would stay home and have the rice and beans ready when they got back.

"What is that music?" Pablo asked as they entered the building. "Is that a radio?"

"No," Papito answered, "that is the orchestra that plays before church-school every Sunday. Not bad, is it?"

Pablo thought it sounded very good and he thought of his drum at home.

When they reached the auditorium, Mr. Everett greeted them, and Pablo was taken to a class of boys his age while Anita went to a class of little girls. Don Romero, Pablo's teacher, had a warm handclasp and a friendly smile.

"Most of us are Puerto Rican, Pablo," Don Romero explained, "and we speak both Spanish and English. I hope you will feel at home."

Pablo did feel at home immediately, thanks to Ernesto and Miguel. These two were friendly right away and explained anything he did not understand.

"Are you going to our school?" Ernesto asked. Pablo told them what grade he had been in in Puerto Rico.

"Yes, you'll go to our school then. Hope you're in the same room with us," Miguel said.

"Who plays in that orchestra?" Pablo asked, when the instruments were tuning up for a special number.

"Anyone who can play well enough. Mr. Pat, that's the director, is very particular, though. Do you play something?"

"Yes, a drum," Pablo said, watching the drummer, an older boy, who could certainly handle those sticks! Pablo wasn't that good, so he was sure he wouldn't have a chance. Maybe he would be good enough someday if he practiced a lot. As he listened to their number he admitted to himself that his island school music had not been nearly that good.

A delicious dinner was waiting for four very hungry people when they got home. After dinner, Don José took money from his pocket and handed it to Pablo. "You remember where we left the subway, don't you, son?" he asked. Yes, Pablo remembered. "Take this to the newsstand on that corner and get *El Diario** and the *Times*. You won't get lost, will you?"

Pablo took the money and put it in his pocket. No, he would not get lost. But he certainly did not much want to go far from home alone. Bingo might be waiting for him if he were not with someone. But he wasn't going to have his family think he was a coward. Maybe Bingo wasn't as mean as he seemed. He had not done anything to him when he returned the apples.

The streets were much quieter than they had been yesterday. Stores were closed and there were fewer cars and trucks. Children were still shouting and playing while parents sat on steps and talked.

As Pablo turned the last corner to the subway, he saw just what he had been dreading. Bingo again, with the two other boys. They were coming toward him this time. Again, they did not seem to see him. Maybe they didn't; maybe he could slip by. But when they reached him, all three swung around and walked along beside him, Bingo on one side and the other two on the other.

"Well, well, if it isn't my friend. Tap and Gus, this guy's called Pablo. That's what I heard his pop call him this morning." Bingo was talking to the two across Pablo as they kept step.

"Hi," both boys said, looking at him out of the corner of their eyes.

"I'm goin' to show yuh something right now, spic, mighty handy, 'cause it will save yuh money.

* A Spanish newspaper, *The Daily*.

See, I'm being very kind, ain't I?" Bingo was trying to speak in a deep man's voice. The other two laughed, a laugh Pablo did not like to hear.

"We ain't goin' nowhere, see," Bingo went on, "but I want to show yuh this stunt. Tap and Gus will stay up here to whistle if any coppers come down. Come on with me."

Pablo was afraid to refuse. Anyway, he knew how to buy the metal piece—that Papa called a "token"—at the window and put it into the turnstile. He'd show Bingo that he already knew. But he didn't want to get on a train. He was thankful that he had some money with him, though this would seem like a big waste, for they weren't going anywhere, as Bingo said.

When the two of them reached the bottom step, Bingo whispered, "Come on around here where the man at the window can't see. Got to be smart and careful, see." They came near the end turnstile. Only a few passengers stood on the platform with their backs to the entrance, waiting for trains. "Quick now. Follow me."

Bingo looked all around to make sure, and then, stooping low, ducked under the turnstile and stood up on the other side. Without looking back, he began sauntering down the platform, whistling. So that was it. Bingo was showing him how to get a ride without paying any money. He might have known. Well, nothing doing! Caught or not caught, it wasn't right and he'd not do it.

Turning on his heel, Pablo walked away from the turnstile and started up the stairs. Some way, he'd get home safely, and this time he was going to tell Papito all about it.

As he was halfway up, he heard running steps down the platform behind him. He hurried. But just as he reached the top step, something grabbed his left heel from behind and he fell heavily on the step, hitting his knee painfully on the iron lift. Bingo passed him with an elaborate, "Pardon me." By the time Pablo had picked himself up and reached the top step, there was no sign of the boys. Pablo began walking slowly and painfully toward home.

A deep voice from behind made him jump. "Hello, Pablo, did you hurt yourself?" Pablo turned to find Patrolman Cruz walking beside him, swinging his stick.

"Not very much. Just a little," Pablo said, more thankful to see Mr. Cruz than he wanted to admit.

"What are you doing down here on this corner, anyway?" the officer asked, walking beside him. Pablo remembered and turned to the newsstand.

"I'm getting papers for Papa," he said. Mr. Cruz waited for him. Then they walked on toward the

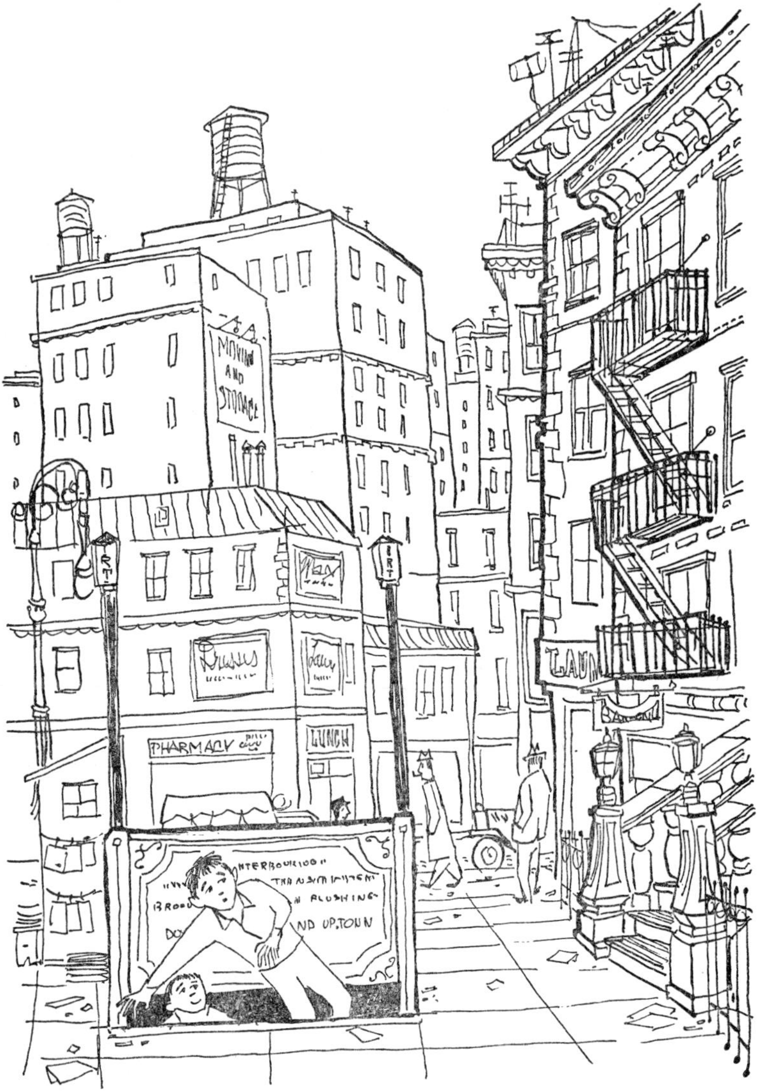
MOVING AND STORAGE
PHARMACY
LUNCH
FLUSHING
UP-TOWN

Torres apartment house in silence until they reached the last corner.

"I'll leave you here, Pablo," the patrolman said, his hand on Pablo's shoulder. "Maybe it is just as well that Bingo and his gang should not think I am taking care of you. I've seen these guys pull their stunts before with new boys in this community and they soon tire of it if the fellow wants to be honest. Don't be afraid of them, Pablo."

Patrolman Cruz's eyes twinkled as he pulled two apples from his pocket. "Take these home and share them with Anita," he said with a grin. Then his face sobered. "I wish we could do something with Bingo and his friends, Pablo. I still hope they will come to PAL some day. But so far they will not believe that I am their friend. Don't forget Friday night. We will be looking for you."

Pablo pocketed the apples, tightened his hold on the papers under his arm and walked on home, whistling.

CHAPTER SEVEN

PABLO BEATS THE DRUM

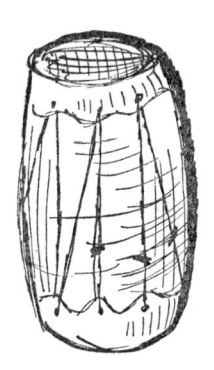

Pablo went to school on Monday by himself. Doña Isabela took Anita, because she was so small. Anyway, Pablo thought, as he put his letter from the island school in his pocket, it would look sissy to have Mama take him at his age.

Children were already gathering and a baseball game was in progress in the playground. He passed through the crowd on the school steps and walked through the hall until he found a teacher. As he hesitated, she smiled and said, "Good morning. Are you new? And are you Puerto Rican?" He nodded. "Then come with me to Miss Sevilla's office." Pablo followed down two hallways to the door marked, "Orientation Office." The teacher led him inside.

"A new boy, Miss Sevilla," she said and left him.

"Ah, *buenos dias.*[*] Be seated and I will be with

---

[*] Good morning.

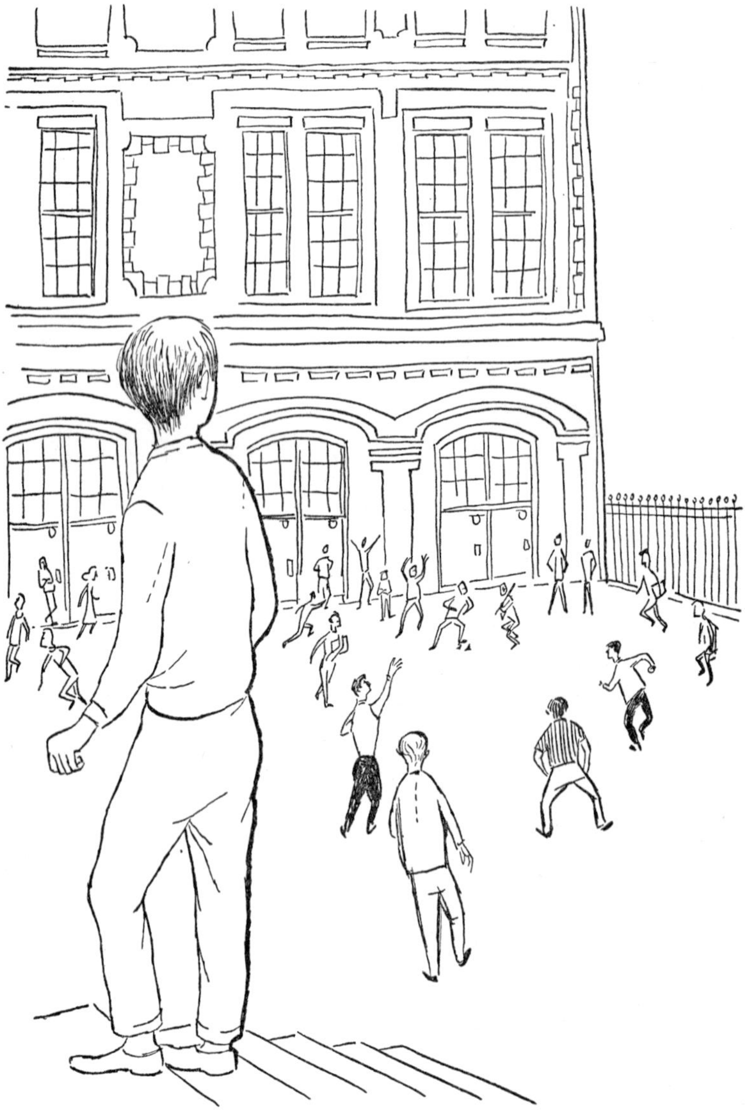

you in a minute," Miss Sevilla said. Pablo thought he had never seen a prettier teacher as he watched her questioning a mother and daughter in Spanish.

When she finished, she turned to Pablo and took the letter he handed her and read it carefully. "When did you come from our island of Puerto Rico?" Miss Sevilla asked in a friendly way. She even said the name of the island as if she loved it.

Pablo told her, and when she asked about his home down there, Pablo talked for ten minutes, telling her all about his school, Calle Agosto, and Hanson House. At last she interrupted.

"Pablo, your English is remarkably good, much better than most of our boys and girls. I think Miss Lester, the principal, will let you go right on with the ninth grade." She looked at the letter again and then said, "I see here that you played a drum in the drum corps in Puerto Rico." Pablo told her he did not think he played very well.

"We do not have a corps here, but we do have an orchestra. It happens that this is the very last day for tryouts. How would you like to try out this afternoon with the rest of the drummers? Shall I give your name to Mr. Stephens, the orchestra director?"

"I did not bring my drum," Pablo answered.

"Oh, the school provides the instruments. You need not bring your own."

Of course, Pablo wanted more than anything else to be in an orchestra. But was he good enough? The idea frightened him and he wished he had more time to think about it and to do some practicing.

"You might as well try, Pablo. Come to the assembly hall right after school. Now I will take you to Miss Lester."

Miss Lester put him in the ninth grade within a few minutes. "You may have a little trouble at first," she said, "but you'll soon catch on," and she left him with his room teacher, Mrs. Henry. The first boys he saw were Miguel and Ernesto, who grinned a welcome to him.

The first day of school went slowly for Pablo. There was so much to get used to. At lunch time, his two new friends took him to the lunchroom, where he walked past a counter and tried to choose food. There was no rice and beans. Miss Thomas had told him this would happen. North Americans do not eat the same things that Puerto Ricans like and he would have to learn to like North American food. He did not much like the vegetable soup and egg sandwich he finally chose with the money Papa had given him. He wondered how Anita was getting along. One thing he was thankful for; he had not seen Bingo, except across the playground.

When the last bell rang at three-thirty, Pablo went reluctantly to the assembly hall, almost hoping no one would call on him. But just after he entered, a big voice called, "All drummers in this corner," and Pablo followed several boys.

"Sit down there, and let's see what you can do, three at a time." Pablo found himself in front of a drum that looked quite different from his.

"Tighten them," Mr. Stephens ordered.

Pablo reached for the ropes but there weren't

any. How could he tighten his drum without the ropes? The other boys seemed to be turning something. "What's the matter there?" the director asked, not unkindly.

"Where are the ropes, sir?" Pablo blurted out.

The other boys laughed. "I see. You aren't used to this kind of drum. Where did you come from?"

"Puerto Rico," Pablo answered, "last week."

"Let's try out these other boys first, then. Some of them played last year and they know these drums."

Pablo's seat was taken by one of the other boys and the tryout began. Three of them were good drummers and he was not surprised when they were chosen immediately, with the other two as substitutes.

"Pablo," Mr. Stephens said in a kindly tone, "learn about these drums and come back when we have another tryout. If you want help, come to my office next Monday. I'm sorry I can't use all of you, but the orchestra is not big enough."

Pablo was glad to start for home.

The quick disappointment over the orchestra stung him. He wished he hadn't gone at all. Of course, he was too new and did not have a chance with the others. It would be a long time before he would be as good as the other boys. He'd have his hands full catching up with school, for the term here had started some time ago and subjects were quite different from those in his island school.

Anita was home when Pablo arrived. She was bubbling over, trying to tell him everything at once, and to show him what she had made from construction paper. It was a fir tree with squirrels in the branches. "My teacher says we will see real squirrels in the park. Some day she will take us for a walk."

Pablo waited until Anita's excitement had run down and she had settled on the sofa with a book. Then he took his drum from its bag, tightened the ropes, and began to work on different rhythms. Anita put her hands to her ears in her usual way, and pretended that the sound hurt her.

"Ay, Mamita, this is terrible. Such a noise." She bounced off the sofa. "I'll go down on the steps a while and watch people. May I?"

Doña Isabela gave her permission, laughing at Anita's apparent ear trouble.

Anita ran to the hall door, pushed it with all her might, and ran smack into something in the outside hall. That something was Bingo! He must have had his face right against the door, for it bumped his head a hard wallop, throwing him against the railing. What in the world was Bingo doing there? Pablo wondered. The boy looked foolish as he picked himself up, rubbing the fast rising lump on his forehead.

"I just stopped close to the door to listen to that thing," Bingo said, pointing to Pablo's drum. "You do pretty good on it. Is it yours?"

This is strange, thought Pablo, but if Bingo wants to talk about a drum he might as well come in.

"Yes," Pablo answered. "Want to try it? Come on in."

Bingo hesitatingly entered the hall, looking around. "Say, you have a nice place. I wish ours looked like this. Huh! It won't, though, now that Mom's not home."

Pablo wished his mother and grandmother could speak English so he did not have to do all the talking. "Where is your mother?"

"Aw, she and my pop don't live together no more. She's working in a hospital. I see your dad around here. He's nice, isn't he?" Pablo nodded.

"My sister don't like me," Bingo went on. "She don't like to do all the cookin' and washin' and ironin' when she comes home from work and she says I keep things messed up like a pig-pen."

Pablo wondered how Bingo stood it, living with a sister who didn't like him. "Who are the two boys you go around with?" Pablo asked. "Tap and Gus."

"Aw, they're in the next grade. I don't like them much but they dare me to do things and it's exciting and something to do. It isn't much fun, though," and then he pointed to the drum. "Say, why don't you play that in the school orchestra?"

"I'm not good enough, not yet," Pablo answered. No use telling him about the tryout.

"You can be some day, I'll bet. Well, I'd better git along before the hollerin' begins upstairs. Be seein' yuh." And Bingo left without looking toward the others.

"Where did you get to know this Bingo?" Doña Isabela asked.

"Oh, here and there, mostly on the street. He lives upstairs." Pablo tried to sound casual.

Now he picked up his drum again and played softly as he kept thinking about Bingo. Would Tap and Gus get Bingo to try other stunts on him, later? Anyway, he decided not to tell Papito about the apples or the subway. He would like Papa to like Bingo.

In school, Pablo found that everyone spoke English so fast he had a hard time understanding things. Mrs. Henry assured him that English would grow easier all the time. One day Miss Sevilla called him into her office to ask how he was getting along. Everyone was trying to be most kind. Ernesto and Miguel came home with him one afternoon, and he would be seeing them at PAL.

At last Friday night came, the big night for him at Ferris Center with the policeman and the boys. In the middle of the week a postcard from Mr. Everett had asked him to come half an hour early and meet him in his office. What could Mr. Everett want with him? Pablo rushed through supper and started for Ferris Center in plenty of time.

"Where do yuh think you're goin'?" a voice asked from behind, and Bingo fell in step with Pablo. Pablo was not afraid, because Bingo was alone.

He told Bingo where he was going. Then he had an inspiration. "Say, come along with me."

"Who, me?" Bingo said in a loud voice. "Say, them coppers don't want me. They don't like me. I get into too much trouble."

"How do you know they don't like you? I heard one say he wished you'd come to PAL."

"A copper said that? How did he know me?"

"You just said you get into trouble, didn't you? But Mr. Cruz said he'd like to have you in PAL."

Bingo walked on in silence for quite a while. They were nearing Ferris Center. "Aw, well," Bingo said at the door, "I guess I might as well go in and see what kind of a joint it is, if you're sure they won't bounce me."

Pablo left Bingo at the gym door and went down the hall to Mr. Everett's office. Mr. Everett was sitting at his desk and there was another man with him.

"Come in, Pablo. Mr. Pat wants to meet you before he goes home to Westchester."

Mr. Pat shook hands with Pablo and told him to sit down. "You like music, don't you, Pablo?" Mr. Pat's keen blue eyes seemed to be centered on him.

"Si, señor," Pablo laughed. "I mean, yes, sir."

"I like to hear Spanish again, Pablo. I had a wonderful time last summer for several weeks hearing it all the time."

There was a silence. Pablo felt as if he ought to be remembering something. Both men were looking at him until he felt embarrassed. Then they exchanged smiles and Mr. Pat went on. "Yes, I saw many interesting things last summer. One of them was a group of boys clearing a banana patch to make a playground. They were all chattering Spanish and I don't think they even saw me on the balcony."

Pablo's mind began to click. Playground—bananas? Why, Mr. Patterson, of course! Both men laughed heartily at the strange look on Pablo's face.

"Yes, I'm Mr. Patterson, Pablo, or Mr. Pat to the crowd around here. Thank you for the nice note you wrote me after Miss Thomas gave you my check. I'm glad it helped out when you needed it. And I am glad you and your family are all here in New York City together."

Pablo was too surprised to speak. The orchestra leader was really Mr. Patterson, who had sent the money for him.

Mr. Everett came to the rescue. "Mr. Patterson gives Ferris Center professional help with our orchestra that you heard on Sunday. He is first violinist in the New York Philharmonic Orchestra. We are the most fortunate people in the world to receive his help and he gives it to us free. That is the kind of man our Mr. Pat is, Pablo."

Mr. Pat interrupted. "Miss Thomas has written me, Pablo, that you are beginning on the drum. How about coming out to orchestra practice next week on Tuesday? I can use another drummer when you are good enough and I'll be glad to help you with the lessons you need. What do you say?"

What could he say? He was still too surprised.

As they walked down the hall together they met Patrolman Cruz. "So that's where you are, Pablo. Time to come with me if Mr. Pat is through with you."

Both men laughed as Mr. Pat took his hand off one of Pablo's shoulders and the policeman put his on the other and hurried him to the gym.

"A miracle has happened, Pablo," Mr. Cruz whispered in his ear. "See who's playing down there? One of your not-so-good friends." Pablo watched Bingo awkwardly trying for baskets and missing every one. "I hope you're better than he is. Are you?" Mr. Cruz asked.

Pablo grinned. "Yes, sir," he said, and then he thought better of it. "Well, maybe," he corrected himself.

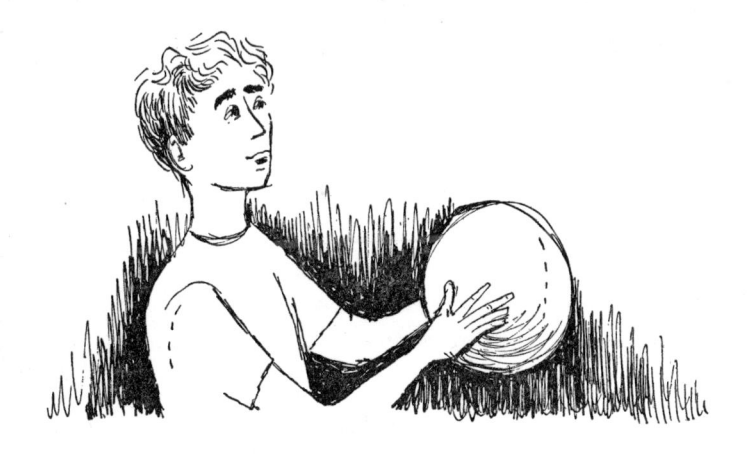

CHAPTER EIGHT

A GIFT FROM ANITA

On the way home from Ferris Center, Bingo was very quiet.

"Them's nice guys, I guess," he said at last. "I liked basketball all right."

"How about going with me next Friday?" Pablo asked.

"Maybe yes, maybe no. I'll see," Bingo answered vaguely, kicking an empty paper sack in front of him down the sidewalk.

"I'm getting a paper route tomorrow, Bingo. Why don't you?"

Pablo thought it might be fun if Bingo would be doing the same things he was after school. It would be a lot better than wandering the streets with Tap and Gus, anyway.

"Me earn dough?" and he almost stopped walking. "What for? That big, lazy Josefina would take it all as soon as I went through our door on pay day. No thanks. That's no good."

"Josefina." So that was Josy's real name.

When they reached his door, Pablo urged, "Well, anyway, I sure hope you come with me next Friday night. With some practice you wouldn't be bad, you know, at basketball. So long," and he closed his door. He could hear Bingo going slowly up the steps and did not envy him his sister's companionship.

"So this is the day you become a newspaper business man, eh son?" Don José said the next morning at breakfast table. "You made arrangements with Mr. Fitzman and know what to do?"

Pablo nodded.

"How long will it take you, son?"

"From four to six every day, if I am fast," Pablo answered.

"When is orchestra practice?" Don José asked.

The question was like a blow in the stomach. How was he going to be at orchestra practice on Tuesdays at five and deliver papers at the same time? Why had he not thought of this problem before?

"That's on Tuesdays, Papito. I'll make arrangements."

His father seemed to give it no further thought and Pablo was glad. But how was he going to do it?

As he walked to the grocery store for supplies for Doña Isabela the problem was all he could think about. How was he going to practice at five o'clock?

"Hiya, Pablo," a voice said behind him, "your ma got to have things to cook, too?" Bingo was grinning in a more friendly way than ever before and Pablo thought it was the first time he had ever heard Bingo use his first name.

"Si, yes, we eat a lot at our house," Pablo answered. Then he knew he might have the answer to his problem. Would Bingo be willing? But first, the groceries. They got their things, and walked out together toward home.

"Bingo, I need help on Tuesday afternoons. If you'll carry my papers from five to six so I can go to orchestra practice, I'll give you—say one and a half times as much as I'll get for those deliveries. Then you'll have some money of your own. How about it?"

Bingo thought a moment. "Josy wouldn't need to know I got any money, would she? She isn't home until six-thirty. What'll I have to do?"

Pablo explained. After he'd delivered today's papers, he'd know how far he could get in an hour. Then he'd let Bingo know which corner to meet him on at five on Tuesdays and Bingo could then finish the deliveries for Pablo. Bingo agreed to try.

"Lucky my route's around Ferris Center. Gee, thanks a lot, Bingo. I'll tell you Monday where to meet me," and Pablo's heart felt light for the first time since breakfast. That hadn't been hard to work out. Sure, he'd lose some money, but it was worth it. Papito had said his money was to be his own for school supplies and he'd manage somehow to get along with a little less.

As Pablo gathered up his papers at Mr. Fitzman's store that afternoon, he wondered if he should explain to Mr. Fitzman about Bingo and Tuesday afternoons. What if Mr. Fitzman did not approve? Why should he know? It was Pablo's business, wasn't it, and what difference was it who took the papers as long as they were delivered? He decided not to tell Mr. Fitzman.

It was pretty tough that first Saturday afternoon, making sure the papers got to the right people. The boy who had had the route before him had gone to a hospital to stay a long time and could not show him the best way to cover the route. Pablo had to figure it out alone.

At one door a little Chinese man handed him two pieces of candy with a friendly smile and Pablo accepted them gratefully. They tasted good as he went on with his papers. He wondered if the little man had ever delivered papers and knew how hungry a boy got.

Tuesday came at last and Pablo hurried with all his might to make the needed deliveries before he met Bingo.

"Good luck, Bingo, and thanks. I'll pay you on Saturday," and Pablo dashed off for Ferris Center.

The orchestra was tuning up when Pablo reached the hall. Mr. Pat motioned him to sit in the front row.

"Watch and listen today, Pablo. I'll give you a little time afterward on the drum."

Then his baton rapped sharply and all the instruments were silent. This was a time that Pablo

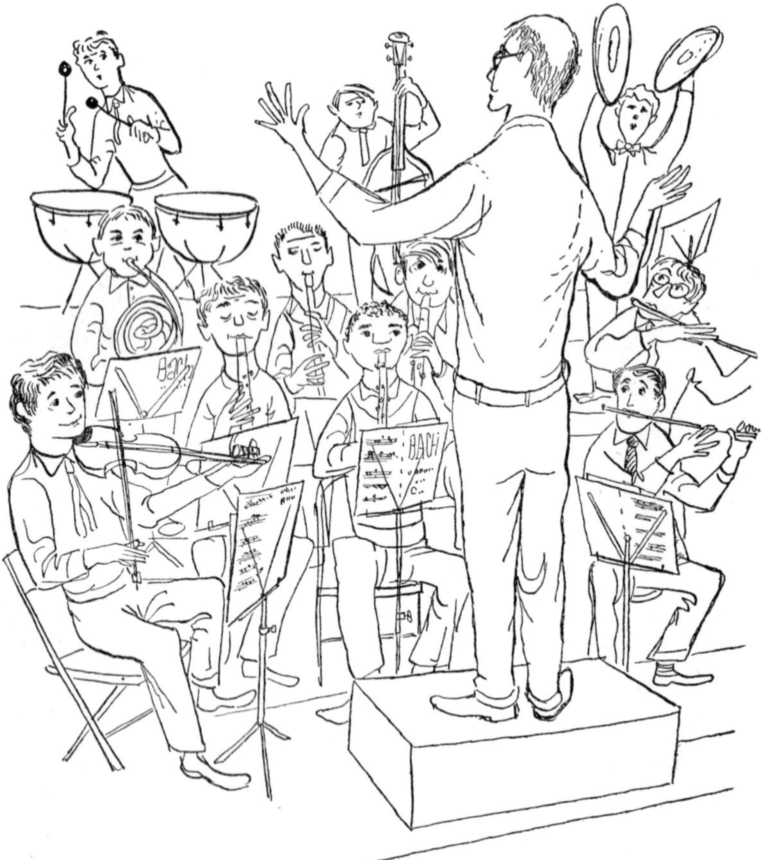
BACH

always liked, just before the real music began. Practice was under way and Pablo watched every movement of the drummer. He was good, all right!

At the end of the hour, instruments were put away and soon Mr. Pat and Pablo were alone. Mr. Pat explained the drum to Pablo, the kind they used that is tightened by screws and has no ropes. Then he had Pablo play for him. After a few rhythms, Pablo said, "I wish I had a new drum like this, Mr. Pat. Some day, I will." He thought of the ten dollars left from Mr. Pat's check.

"How much are they, Mr. Pat?"

"Around twenty-five dollars and up," Mr. Pat answered. "But for now you can still practice on your old one. I think you will be a real drummer some day, Pablo."

Such praise from Mr. Pat made Pablo tingle with pride.

"I have a reason for wanting you to work hard now. Christmas is coming soon and we're having a play of the nations, showing how Christmas is celebrated around the world. In several places a drum is needed, especially in the African scene. Our drummer is going away for the holidays. Do you think you can be ready by Christmas to do a good job for me?"

Could he? Of course!

Pablo walked on air as he went home that night. Everything seemed to be going just right, so why shouldn't he whistle and jump over cracks in the sidewalk and bound up the apartment house stairs three at a time?

And so he burst into the apartment that night without the least idea of what he would find within those four walls of home. He soon found out. A strong, sweet odor met him as he opened the door. Not anything cooking, he knew. Where did it come from? Then he saw them. Beautiful big red roses in a pitcher on the kitchen table.

"Wow! Where did those come from?" he shouted. But no voice answered and no one seemed to be around.

"Where's everyone?" he called again.

"In here, son. Come in." It was Grandmother's voice from the bedroom. Pablo stood in the doorway and looked at the three of them, Mamita, Anita, and Grandmother. Mamita and Anita were sitting on the bed close together and Grandmother was sitting on a chair. All looked frightened. Anita was crying, with her head in Mamita's lap.

"What has happened? Tell me." Pablo was

frightened, too. Was something wrong with Papa?

"The flowers, son, the roses. Anita stole them," Mamita said at last.

"Anita—stole—roses?" Pablo was sure he had not heard right.

"I'll tell you, Pablito," Grandmother said. "Anita was down on First Avenue. She saw big cans of flowers on the sidewalk against the side of the house. When she did not see any store, she thought someone was giving them away, that she could help herself. And so, poor little thing, she brought that bunch to us. She did not mean to steal. But no one gives flowers away, not in New York. We know that. These must cost much money. What shall we do? Maybe someone followed her home and knows."

This brought a fresh flood of tears from Anita.

"Where's Papa?" Pablo asked.

"This is the night he works. He will not be home until tomorrow night," Mamita said.

By this time Anita was clinging to Pablo, crying against his sleeve.

"I didn't mean to, Pablo, but they were so beautiful. I wanted them for us here. They look like the ones Miss Thomas has in her garden, don't they? I didn't steal, did I, Pablo?"

How Pablo wished for Papa to tell them what to do. He was afraid to take time to go down to Ferris Center. He went to the front window and looked into the street. No one was there looking up at their apartment. Of course not, he thought. The owner of the flower shop would wait until tomorrow morning and then send the police. On the other hand, perhaps no one knew Anita had stolen the flowers and they would never hear anything about it. The flowers would wither and be thrown out and that would be all there would be to it. Should he just wait and see and do nothing?

"No, you can't do that, Pablo. Your family are honest people. You do not steal nor lie. Do something about this right now." It was almost like his own voice speaking to him, though no one had said a word.

"Anita, you come on with me. We'll be back soon, Mamita. Don't worry."

He went to his drawer and got all the money he had, the ten-dollar bill from Mr. Pat's money that he was saving for Christmas. Taking Anita by the hand, he led her to the street.

"I'm afraid, Pablo. What will they do to me? Where are we going?"

"I don't know what they will do, little sister, but we will see. We are going to the shop. Just keep hoping the flower man is a kind man and does not hate Puerto Ricans."

"No one hates me at school, Pablo. Everyone is nice to me." She squeezed her brother's hand. He pressed it in return.

"I'm glad, little sister. You keep on making them like you."

It had been dark for some time. Days were getting shorter now. Stores were closed or closing with great banging of doors and shutters and shopkeepers were saying goodnight to each other in many languages as they passed. Pablo felt the first coolness of Fall blow down First Avenue as they walked along, and he pulled the collar of his cotton shirt together. He felt a shudder run through Anita and put his arm protectingly across her shoulders to keep her warm.

"There is the place, Pablo, right there," she said. "Against that wall they stood. Cans and cans of them. Hundreds, I'll bet. There were all kinds and no one was sitting there to sell them. But they're all gone now."

They stopped while Pablo looked the situation over. It was a florist's shop, all right, facing First Avenue on the corner. Evidently, whoever was selling the flowers on the street had stepped inside at the moment Anita came along. Looking at the dark sign outside, Pablo realized that the shop was closed for the night.

"There's nothing we can do now, Anita. It's too late. The store's closed. Nothing to do but go home and go to bed. I have money to pay for the flowers and—well, if he's a kind man, it may be all right. But you must never, never take anything again without paying for it, little sister. Promise?"

"Yes, you know I promise," Anita answered in a low voice. "I'll never never do it again, Pablo. You're the most wonderful brother and I won't make any more fun of your drum playing. I don't really mind it at all."

Pablo was able to smile a little in the dark as he led his sister home.

CHAPTER NINE

FIRE BUGS

Pablo was restless all night, wondering between dreams what tomorrow would bring. The little family was very quiet at breakfast and did not seem to be hungry.

As Pablo, with Anita, started out again for the florist shop, he found her little hand very cold. There was no jumping around this morning and no whistling. They walked in silence, and each step seemed to Pablo to be bringing them near something serious and he wished they were running the other way.

At last they reached the florist's corner. The door of the shop was open. A gray-haired man was setting cans of flowers on the sidewalk where Anita said they had been yesterday. The two stood behind him as he pushed the cans this way and that and arranged blossoms in several of the cans. Would he never see them? Suddenly he turned, and almost stepped on them.

"Mister, did you lose any flowers yesterday?" Pablo began. "I mean, did any disappear from here?" He pointed to the sidewalk.

The man frowned. "What? I don't understand. What do you two want this early in the morning?"

Pablo had to begin again. At last the story was out. Here was his ten dollars if the man would not arrest Anita because she did not mean to steal—

The man was listening closely and looking from one to the other.

"You're Puerto Rican, aren't you?"

"*Si, señor,*" Pablo answered, not realizing he spoke in Spanish.

"*Bueno, y yo tambien,*"* the man answered and he smiled broadly. "And we have flowers all year in the beautiful gardens of our beloved island, don't

* Good, and I am, too.

we, children? We give them away just as little sister here thought people in New York do." He looked off down the street and took a long breath. "Every house table has its bright bouquet and at night, ah, at night the air is filled with sweet jasmine and lady-of-the-night. Ay, yes, yes," and he took a long breath again, "I grow homesick for my Aguadilla."

Aguadilla? Why, they drove through that town on their way to San Juan. Pablo remembered the many flowers on porches and in the gardens he could see through the fences.

"But here, we pay and pay for every flower." The man looked at the ten dollars Pablo held. "So I will take just the cost of the roses. They are a dollar and a half. Now, my name is Don Antonio," he continued, as he handed Pablo the change, "and if you ever want to buy flowers, remember Don Antonio. But for now, if Anita will come sometimes on Saturday nights at six, I will give her a few blossoms to take to her mamita, flowers that will not keep in the shop over Sunday. Those Sundays you will have flowers to remind you of our beautiful Borinquen, with the love of Don Antonio."

Again the children were silent as they walked home, but it was very different this time. Pablo wondered if Anita was as grateful for kind people as he was. Grandmother and Mamita almost cried when the children told them about Don Antonio and Aguadilla and the dollar-fifty only.

"Of course he was kind. Is he not from Puerto Rico?" Mamita said. But Grandmother answered quickly, "Not because he is from one place or another, daughter, is anyone kind, but because kindness is in his heart toward all peoples. Children, remember today well, and be kind to everyone, always."

That was like Grandmother, Pablo thought, always being kind to everyone. But he wondered how she would act if she had to deal with Gus and Tap—and Bingo, too.

Before leaving for school, Pablo went upstairs to get the bag for his papers. Bingo had said he would leave it in a corner of the dark hallway when he returned Tuesday night and Pablo could get it whenever he was ready. Now, as he passed Bingo's door, he heard boys talking inside and recognized the voices of Gus and Tap. What could they be up to early in the morning? Where was Josy? Then he remembered that she left for work at seven.

"Sure I can. I'm not afraid of nothin'," Gus was saying. "Youse guys fix the rags. Plenty of stuff on 'em, understand, right under them steps."

"How'll yuh do it 'n not get caught?" Bingo asked, and his voice sounded shaky.

"Aw, leave it to me, see! It'll be an accident. That place is no good, nohow. Needs cleanin' out."

"We'll be real fire bugs, like the big guys, once we honest do one. I read a lot about it in the paper. Them guys got nerve." That was Tap's voice.

Pablo did not dare stand at the door longer. He picked up his bag and walked away. What were fire bugs? People who put out fires? Pablo wondered as he went into the Torres apartment. Whatever it was, Pablo didn't trust Tap and Gus and he felt sure Bingo was being forced into something he didn't want to do. Why didn't they leave Bingo alone? He wasn't bad at all when they weren't around.

But Pablo wanted to get off for school before they came down and so wasted no time in gathering his books and leaving.

Wednesday passed quickly in school. There was a high wind as Pablo left the building at three-thirty and he almost dreaded the paper route that lay before him. Ernesto and Miguel walked part way home with him. They had been at PAL last Friday and complimented Pablo on his basketball.

"I'll bet you make the team for Ferris Center," Ernesto said, and since he was captain, Pablo felt pretty good.

"How about Bingo?" Miguel asked and both boys laughed.

"What makes him think he can play basketball?" Ernesto asked. "I never saw worse."

Then they saw that Pablo was not laughing.

"No, he isn't good. But, fellows, it's something that he came last week. I hope he comes again. He liked it all right last Friday," Pablo said.

"Sure, sure, we hope so, too. He's not such a bad guy away from Tap and Gus," Miguel said.

"You know them, too, then?" Pablo asked.

"Sure, who doesn't? They're the worst bums around here. Even Patrolman Cruz can't do anything with them but keep watch on them."

What would Ernesto and Miguel say if he told them what he had heard this morning?

It was after six by the time Pablo finished delivering his papers and night had come. The wind was at his back, cold and biting, and almost carried him down the street. He thought of the hurricanes at home in Puerto Rico and was thankful that such storms did not hit New York. At least he had never heard of one.

Pablo was within three blocks of home when there came from behind him the sound of bells, and heavy trucks and cars pulled to a stop along the sides of the street. Pablo had seen and heard fire engines before. They always filled him with excitement and terror. But he had never seen a fire. The engines always disappeared far down the street and it had been no use to run after them.

But tonight it was different. The trucks were not going fast. He saw them turn to the left. Was that his street? Pablo began to run. As he rounded the corner he found excited and confused people blocking the street in front of his home. The house across the narrow street was on fire. Waves of red flames shot from the second-floor windows. Police blocked his way and he could not get home. Would the flames reach across the street, too? Where were Mamita and Grandmother and Anita? Terrible fear gripped Pablo.

Hoses were now pouring water onto the fire. A fireman was carrying someone down a ladder from the third floor, while the fire escape was black with

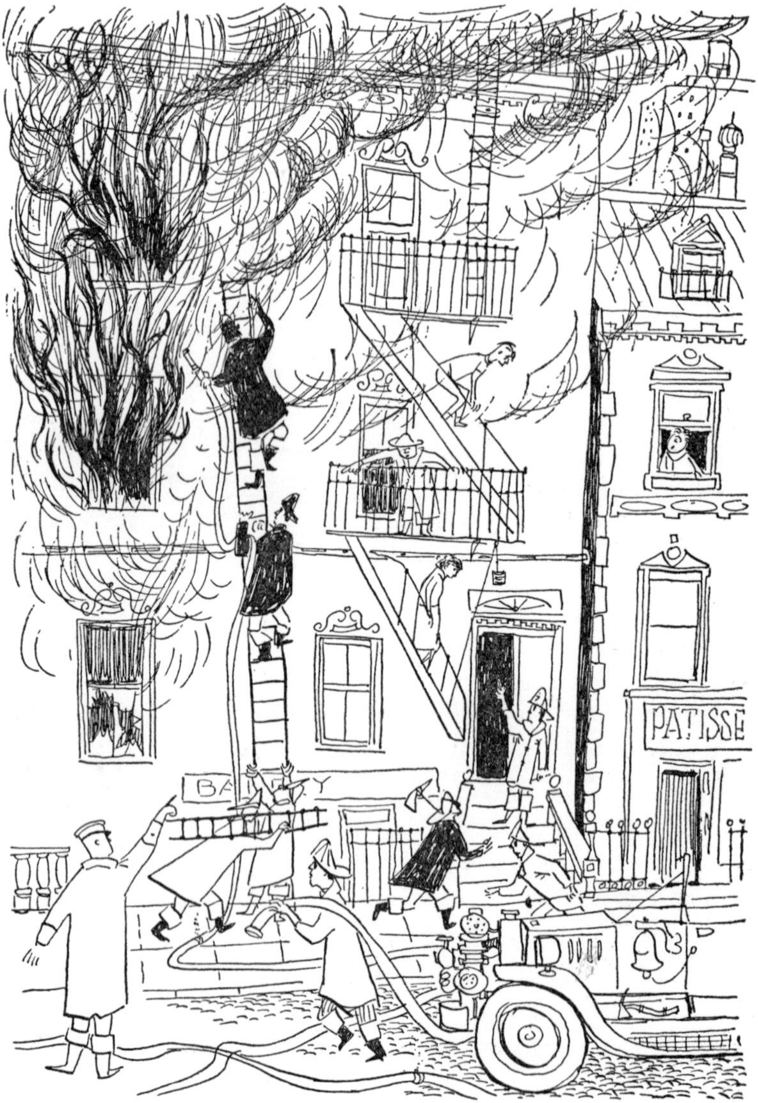
PATISSE

people. The last part of the ladder, that had hung above the sidewalk and so mystified Pablo that first day they arrived, reached the sidewalk now under the weight of the people escaping.

Almost in Pablo's ear a tremendous voice shouted with authority, "Stretch the net. There's someone on the roof. Stretch the net, here!"

A huge net was held by firemen in the street and the loud voice shouted to the black figure silhouetted on the roof against the sky. "Jump! Jump! Hey, jump from that roof!"

For an instant the body seemed to be flying through the air. The next moment it hit the net with such force that it bounced twice. Then it lay still, only a short distance from Pablo.

The voice in front continued orders, "Take him to the hospital. He's probably all right," and the limp body was carried out of sight.

By this time there was more smoke than flames coming out and the excitement was dying down. Pablo thought he could see Mamita at their window, leaning out. In a few minutes he was allowed to pass and rushed up the stairs and through their door. As he turned to close the door, he jumped at the sight of Bingo and Tap and Gus rushing up the steps as fast as they could go. All three looked frightened and no one spoke to him, though they must have known his door was open.

Mamita and the other two were all right, though shaken by the experience.

"And we didn't know where you were, Pablo, and we wanted you here with us. I feel safe when you're home, Pablito. Please stay." And Anita looked at him from a very pale little face.

"Of course, silly little one, I'm home to stay. Don't worry. It's all over now."

"What started the fire, I wonder. Did anyone on the street say?" Mamita asked.

"No," Pablo answered slowly.

"Who knows?" Grandmother said. "Maybe boys with matches or cigarettes. Probably just an accident."

Accident? Boys? Pablo felt cold and sick. He stared a long time at the arithmetic book open before him. Was that what Tap and the others had been talking about this morning? What was a fire bug, anyway?

CHAPTER TEN

THE AWARD

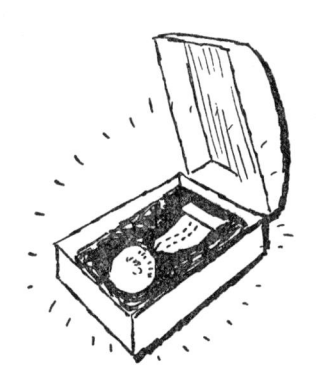

Two weeks passed and Pablo had told no one what he had heard at Bingo's door that morning or given any hint that he might know what started the fire across the street. No one had asked him, of course. Maybe if he had actually seen the boys setting the fire he would have felt that he must tell someone, at least Patrolman Cruz. So he thought. But what if the gang went on and on, setting fire to more houses? They might even set fire to their own, only surely Bingo would not burn his own apartment house. There had been no more fires up to now, but Pablo was not happy with his thoughts.

Today was assembly day at school. Mrs. Henry, his teacher, had said this would be a very special day. Pablo could hardly wait for the ten o'clock gong to sound.

The school orchestra was playing a lively tune as the boys entered the big assembly hall and Pablo felt like skipping down the aisle instead of walking. Wouldn't it be funny if everyone, even the teachers, came in skipping today? He laughed out loud. Ernesto, beside him, looked at him questioningly and then he laughed, too.

"You're a funny guy, Pablo. Sometimes you're serious as an old judge. Then, suddenly, everything's funny. You're nuts!"

The boys had just sat down when someone tapped Pablo on the shoulder. Miss Lester was leaning over him.

"Pablo, please come into my office for a few minutes," she said. Pablo hated to miss a minute of the assembly. What did she want? Would she scold him for something? If she did, it would be the first time.

In the corner of the office sat a boy and his mother. Miss Lester motioned Pablo to a seat.

"Miss Sevilla is in the other school today and I want your help in her place, as interpreter, Pablo."

Then she turned to the mother. "Mrs. Alvarez, this is Pablo from Puerto Rico. He will interpret for us."

Mrs. Alvarez' eyes lighted up when Pablo translated what Miss Lester had said. Then she poured out her story in a torrent of Spanish. They had come from Puerto Rico last week. Arturo, her son, was in the seventh grade. Miss Lester nodded. She remembered when Arturo had entered. But he was afraid to try to speak English though he knew a good deal. The other boys were picking on him, teasing him, and sometimes fighting him. Mrs. Alvarez wanted

Miss Lester to put a stop to it, and right away.

Miss Lester's smile was kindly.

"Tell her, Pablo, that I understand her problem. It is not new to us. Almost all Spanish-speaking children have to get used to school in New York. I know it is hard at first."

Mrs. Alvarez continued to look down at her rough, red hands.

"But tell her," Miss Lester went on, "that Arturo's teacher understands, too, and will do her best to help him. As for the other boys, they will soon like him and accept him if he doesn't give them reason not to."

While Pablo translated, Arturo was looking at him out of the corner of his eye. I'll bet he's a fighter, all right, Pablo thought. He probably gives the first punches because he isn't sure what they're talking about and he's scared.

When Mrs. Alvarez was satisfied and had left, Miss Lester thanked Pablo and told both boys to go back to the hall.

Pablo asked Arturo where he lived and found it was only two doors from his own house.

"I can lick any kid, understand?" Arturo boasted as they walked down the hall.

"Sure you can, but what's the use? How about our going home together after school?"

"Okay," Arturo answered, still sullen, as they entered the hall. A strange man was speaking from the platform.

"This award may be won by any boy or girl in this school," he was saying. "Your teachers will be the judges at the end of the year. At commencement exercises the Board of Education, which I represent, will present the award to one of you as the Outstanding Citizen of this school."

Everyone clapped. "And now, I want to ask a former pupil of this school, one who won this same award many years ago, to speak. Mr. Wu Ling."

A short man rose and came to the speaker's table.

"My fellow citizens," he began. Pablo looked closely. Where had he seen Mr. Ling before? He knew right away that he liked him. Oh yes, candy, and newspapers! His first long day on the route.

"One of the happiest days of my life was the time I got this award when I was a school boy like all of you. I do not know why I got it, for I was an ordinary boy come recently from China. I loved this land of freedom and opportunity where even the poorest can make something of himself if he tries and is not afraid of work. Good Citizenship to me means cooperation with those about you, with your school and community. It means standing up for the best man for office, when you are old enough to vote. It means helpfulness to others, wherever you are. It means originality and loyalty in meeting problems and, above all, it means true honesty at all times. These are only a few things that make up good citizenship. Oh yes, I should mention grades right now, for that is your business these days. Dear Miss Lester, I almost forgot grades. Shall I be punished?" and he bowed ceremoniously to Miss Lester, who was now seated on the platform. Miss Lester nodded enthusiastically and everyone laughed and clapped as Mr. Ling sat down.

As they went back to their home rooms, Pablo was thinking that that last let him out, all right. He was having a hard time with written English and he knew that even if he could qualify in other ways, his grades would not be good enough. It would be pretty wonderful for the one who did win.

"Was that good news, Pablo?" Mrs. Henry asked as he passed her at their door.

"Yes, I guess, for someone. Not for me," and he took his seat.

"Why not?" Mrs. Henry asked.

Pablo grinned. "Well, first place, grades, Mrs. Henry. I wouldn't have much chance, would I, with a D in English just yesterday?"

Mrs. Henry was looking over his head at the rest of the children coming into the classroom and said absentmindedly, "Grades aren't the only thing."

She knows I'd have no chance, but doesn't want to say so, Pablo thought. For the time being, he dismissed the whole matter. It was time to struggle with another English composition.

As the day wore on, however, Pablo found himself thinking frequently about the award. In fact, he thought of little else during the late afternoon study hour. Wouldn't his family be proud of him if he should ever win such a thing? He was proud of being an American citizen, all right, just as his father and mother and grandmother were. His grandmother had chosen to become an American citizen, he knew, back in 1917 when she could have

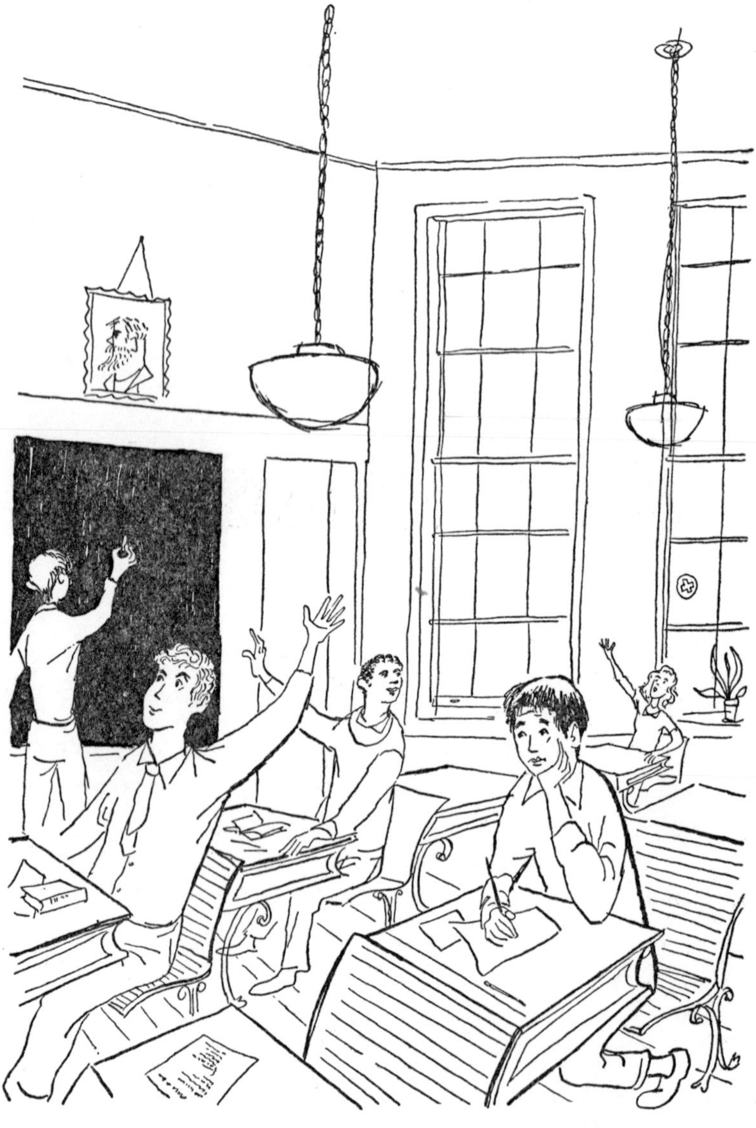

stayed a citizen of Spain. Yes, he was proud of his grandfather's and grandmother's choice that made him a citizen now. But how could he prove to others how he felt?

Then he thought of the fire. Should a good citizen go to the police and tell what he knew, what he had heard through a closed door when he could not even see the people talking? The thought was frightening. What if Gus and Tap and Bingo went to prison because he told on them?

As he walked home with Arturo that afternoon, he was so busy thinking about his problem that he could hardly make himself listen to what the smaller boy was saying.

"They make fun of my name, those Yankees. I'll show them," and Arturo doubled up his fist. Just then Bingo joined them.

"Who's your friend, Pablo?" he asked, jerking a thumb toward Arturo.

"His name's Art and he *is* my friend. He just came from Puerto Rico," Pablo answered.

"Yeah, I know. He's near my room at school. Why doesn't he talk better English?"

"He will, in time. I'll bet your dad didn't speak English when he first came from Italy, did he?"

"I don't know. Maybe not. But your dad does."

"Not when he first came up here, he didn't, very well. They were mean to him at the hotel at first."

"Sure. Josy told me. She works at the same place, you know. They say your dad's an all right guy, now, though."

That was the first time that Pablo knew that Josy worked at his father's hotel.

"He's always been all right. It was just that others couldn't understand him at first. Say, Bingo, why don't you and the other fellows in your class give this kid a chance? He thinks all you want to do is fight and so he's ready to fight. But where'll that get you?"

Bingo had no answer so they walked on in silence. Arturo stayed carefully on the side away from Bingo. They came to Arturo's house first.

"*Adios,*" he said as he left them, and the other two said "*adios*" together.

Bingo gave a funny chuckle. "Imagine me speaking Spanish," he said.

"Well, isn't good-bye *adio* in Italian? They're really the same, almost," Pablo answered.

"Sure, I guess it is," Bingo said. "Gee, we're all mixed up, aren't we?" and both boys laughed.

Pablo had to hurry to get his route started for it was late. He knew Mr. Fitzman wanted those papers out on time. Otherwise the customers complained. As Pablo entered the shop, he found Mr. Fitzman scowling at him from behind the counter.

"Say, young man, I have something to say to you! I've heard something that I don't like."

Was it anything about the fire? Pablo felt his face go pale.

"Someone on your paper route told me that it wasn't you at all, a couple of days ago, who delivered her paper, but another boy. How do you explain that?"

Tuesday! Bingo! The only thing to do was to explain it all. This Pablo did, with a thick throat blocking his words and a pounding in his left side that nearly choked him. Evidently Mr. Fitzman was very angry.

"But you know you made out an application and gave me references. We didn't just pick you off the street. We're careful who carries our papers and this Bingo hasn't much reputation around here. You know that, don't you?"

Pablo nodded. "Why didn't you ask me first?" Mr. Fitzman continued.

"I guess I was afraid you might say no, Mr. Fitzman," Pablo answered weakly.

"You're right. I would have."

He stood for what seemed hours and stared at Pablo. At last he said, "Go on with your papers now and stop here after you finish. I'll still be open."

Pablo shouldered his heavy load and went into the cold street.

CHAPTER ELEVEN

PATROLMAN CRUZ TAKES A HAND

Good citizenship award, indeed! The very thought was bitter to Pablo now as he pushed his way against the cold wind, his bag of papers bumping uncomfortably against his leg. Look at what he had done! He'd made Mr. Fitzman mad enough so that maybe he'd take his route away from him. He guessed he knew all the time that he should not have made his own plans that way. Mr. Fitzman was boss, after all.

The route seemed endless this afternoon and he wondered if he would find a new boy at the paper store when he got back, waiting to take his papers after this.

Finally, he had only a few papers left. Street lights were coming on as he went into the last apartment building. The good odor of onions and frying potatoes and meat crept from under the doors and hit Pablo right in the face. But, somehow, he did not feel as if they would taste good right now. He still had Mr. Fitzman to face.

On the steps leading to the fourth floor, he heard a peculiar sound coming through the transom of a third-floor apartment. It was someone choking and crying at the same time, the way Anita did once when she was sick down in Puerto Rico. Pablo stopped. The sound was frightening. While he stood there the apartment door flew open and a woman rushed into the hall and looked down the stairway. Then she heard Pablo's step above and a wild torrent of Spanish brought him running to her side. Her little girl was terribly sick. Croup. Please, please go for inhalation medicine, and she pushed into his hand a paper with the name of a drug store six blocks away and the name of the medicine.

"But, señora, a store closer will do, won't it?" he asked.

"No, boy, no, only there do they know me and only there they will give you the medicine without money. I have no money now. Run, run fast!"

As he tore down the stairs, Pablo remembered that he had a dollar of his own in his pocket. There was a drug store on a corner two blocks away. If he had to go six blocks each way he might be too late if the little girl was as sick as she sounded. Dropping his paper bag in the entry door, Pablo began running as fast as he could. He thrust the paper into the hand of the surprised druggist, point-

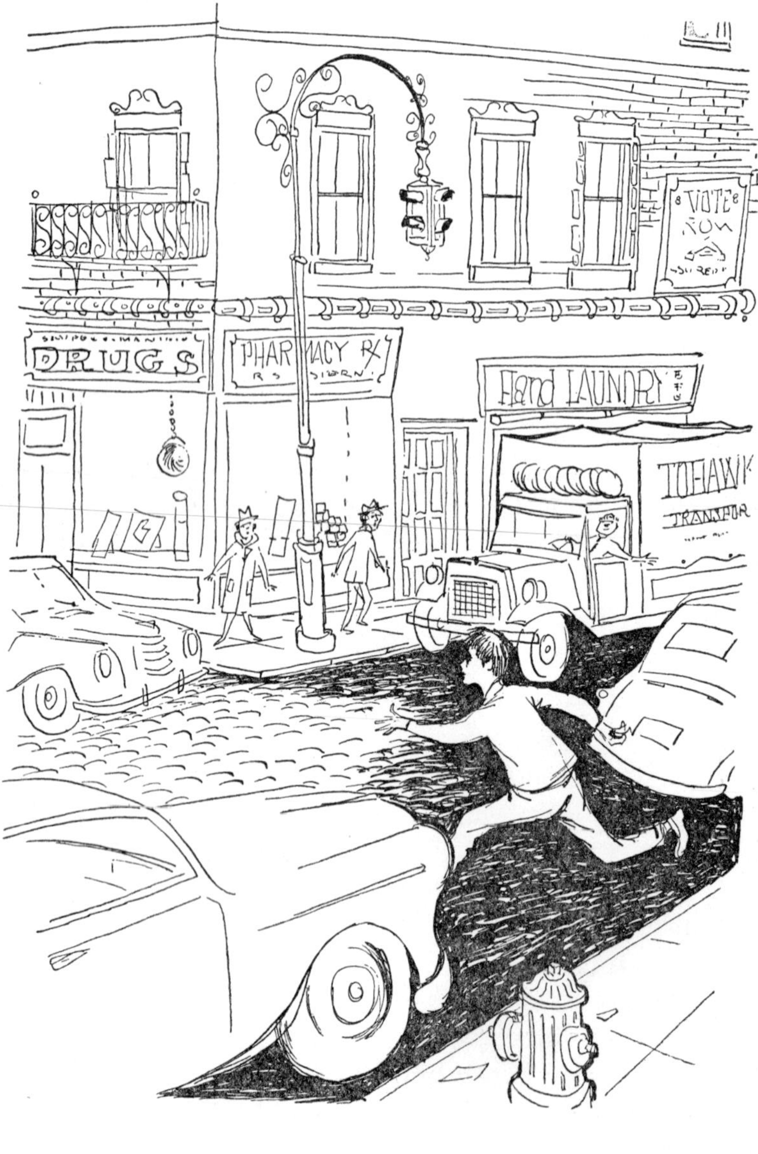
DRUGS
Hand LAUNDRY
VOTE

ing to the name of the medicine. In a few minutes the man handed him a bottle and took seventy-five cents out of his dollar.

The same sounds as before were coming from the apartment as he rushed up the steps and opened the door. He handed the bottle to the woman. Then he stood with his back against the closed door, wondering if he could be any more help. In one corner was a child's bed and over one end stood an opened umbrella. A blanket was stretched across the umbrella like a tent. The choking sound came from under the umbrella. With quick movements, the woman poured some of the medicine into a steaming teakettle that stood on a table hot plate beside the bed. Then she pulled the blanket over the whole table so that the steam would go under the umbrella. Yes, that was what Mamita had done for Anita that time, and she was soon better. A strong, penetrating odor filled the room. Gradually the choking lessened. At last, the woman looked up at Pablo and gave him a faint, tired smile.

"Oh, how can I thank you, angel of God? May God reward you," she said.

Pablo felt sure there was nothing more he could do and so, saying good-bye, he returned to the neglected papers.

How much time had he lost? He had no idea. What would Mr. Fitzman say to his being so late? He was tired and bewildered and wondered why everything had to happen to him at once.

To Pablo's relief and surprise, he saw by a store clock that he was not very late after all. What a lot can happen in a few minutes, he thought, as he ran toward Mr. Fitzman's store. His black hair hung wet on his forehead and he arrived breathless.

"Well, here you are, Pablo. Why the running? I thought you Puerto Ricans always moved slowly."

Pablo told him briefly what had happened, omitting the fact that he had spent his own money for the medicine. That would not interest Mr. Fitzman. Then Pablo took the offered chair.

Mr. Fitzman sat at his counter in silence for a moment and looked closely at Pablo so that the boy finally felt uncomfortable. Why didn't he just say it and have it over with?

"Pablo, I've been thinking this business over. I appreciate your interest in the orchestra and all that, but you should have come to me and talked the thing over, and certainly you should not have given any part of your route to anyone else without asking me."

"Yes sir, I know that now. I'm sorry."

"Patrolman Cruz was just in here. I talked it over with him. He advises me to let Bingo go on with your route on Tuesdays. I find Mr. Cruz's advice always good, Pablo, and so am willing to take it this time."

"Oh, thank you, Mr. Fitzman. I know Bingo will do all right."

"Okay, Pablo," and Mr. Fitzman handed him a magazine in Spanish. "Take this to your folks. They might like it."

Pablo took it, thanked him again, and went

out into the night. Patrolman Cruz had again proven himself a friend, as always. As Pablo started slowly homeward he was thinking about the patrolman and his friendship for all the boys. Then he began wondering if the officer would claim him, Pablo, as a friend, if he knew what Pablo was not telling him.

Suddenly, Pablo turned squarely around and walked back to the store.

"Please, Mr. Fitzman, in which direction did Patrolman Cruz go when he left here?"

"Why, he said something about going to Kall's Place for supper," the storekeeper replied.

Pablo went down the side street until he reached the little restaurant and there, inside the window, sat Patrolman Cruz. Pablo slipped in beside him and, seeing that he had finished his supper, asked if he could talk with him a few minutes. The kindly policeman seemed to understand without further explanation and led Pablo to the back of the place where they could be alone.

"Sure, son, what's on your mind?" the officer asked, his hand on Pablo's knee as if to reassure him.

"Mr. Cruz, I want to tell you what I heard the other day before that fire across from our apartment house," and Pablo told all that was said through the closed door as well as he could remember.

The officer looked serious, and said nothing for a few minutes. Then he spoke.

"Pablo, I need you to do something for me. It will not be easy. I want you to tell Bingo that you heard them. Don't tell all three, just Bingo. Then come tell me how he acted. Until you do this, I cannot do anything. Yet, something must be done. I am mighty afraid for those boys."

Pablo nodded and his head felt like an iron ball. What would happen when he faced Bingo?

Then he remembered that this was Friday night, PAL night, and Bingo had promised to go with him to Ferris Center.

Pablo was so silent at supper that Anita asked what was the matter and to keep her from worrying he tried to joke and laugh. He jumped when the knock came at the door.

"Hey, Pablo, let's go if we're goin'," Bingo called from the hall, though the hour was early.

When they were out on the street, Bingo said, "I wish Tap and Gus'd come, too, but they think no one wants 'em. I told 'em it was okay and they'd have fun shootin' them baskets and maybe playin' a little with them other guys. But they won't. Maybe, if you keep after 'em, they will some time."

Pablo was glad Bingo was talking about Gus and Tap. It was easier to start.

"Bingo, I've got to tell you something. You remember the first night you took my route? It was the day before the fire across the street. The next morning I went to get my bag—" and he told Bingo all he had heard. There was silence when he finished and the noise of their shoes on the pavement sounded like hammers to Pablo.

At last Bingo spoke. "Snoopin', weren't yuh?"

"No, I wasn't, really. I couldn't help but hear as I passed. Maybe I should have gone right on, but somehow I couldn't, because I felt they were making you do something bad. Were they?"

"Ah, well, it's all over now," Bingo answered. They walked on in silence again. Pablo wondered if that was all Bingo was going to say. It would not be much to report to Patrolman Cruz.

"They won't want to do nothin' like that, again," Bingo finally went on; "that scared 'em plenty, the bums, seein' that there fire. Yeah, it sure scared me, too."

"What scared you?" Pablo asked, not knowing what else to say.

"Why, seein' that there real fire across the street. Course, the little old empty shack we was goin' to set fire to wasn't worth nothin', really. But after watchin' all them people jumpin' from the roof like that—well, we changed our minds. What if the shack we set fire to caught places where people live. That would be bad. We wouldn't want that for nothin'."

"Gee, I'm glad," Pablo said and knew Bingo did not know how much he was glad for. So they hadn't set the fire across the street. They hadn't set any fire to anything so there would not be anything that Patrolman Cruz would have to do to the boys.

"Race you to the Center," Pablo shouted and they were off like a shot through the cold night air.

CHAPTER TWELVE

CHRISTMAS

Real winter came at last, the time of year that Pablo and the Torres family both dreaded and yet looked forward to. The first icy morning meant great excitement. Rain fell the night before and now long, clear icicles hung outdoors from the tops of the window frames.

"Hurry, Anita, I don't want to be late for school," Pablo called as he started out the door. He heard his sister's step right behind him.

"Wow! Look at our breath!" Pablo said when they reached the street. He opened his mouth as wide as he could and let out all the breath that was in him. Anita trotted along beside him, busy with something in her hands. Pablo looked down.

"Why, you little idiot, what are you carrying those for?"

"I've got ice sticks, Pablo. I'm taking them to school to show my teacher," Anita answered.

Her brother stopped deadstill. "How silly can you be, Anita? I never heard of a crazier idea. That's just ice. It will melt as soon as you get to school."

"And so? Who's to stop me, mister smarty, anyway?" Anita answered, mischievously. How American she is, already, Pablo thought. "Mister Smarty," indeed! Anita skipped on beside him, changing the icicles from one hand to the other and now and then knocking off an end that shattered into bits on the pavement.

"I'll bet no one has as pretty ice sticks as these. No, they won't have. No, they won't have!" she chanted. Pablo knew there was no use arguing.

School grew more and more interesting and Pablo found his work, even English, easier as weeks passed. He wished his grades were better but Don José never scolded when he brought home his grade card. For that he was thankful.

These days he was often called into Miss Lester's office on the days when Miss Sevilla was in the other school to help with translating for some new and frightened or belligerent newcomer. One morning after such an interview, Miss Lester asked Pablo to wait.

"You're a great help to me, Pablo. I like the way you make friends with even those who are most difficult for me to handle. They are soon smiling at you, I notice. I am pretty sure you had something to do with civilizing that little Arturo in seventh grade. How did you do it?"

Pablo grinned at her. "What did you do?" she persisted.

Pablo didn't know exactly. What could he say? He'd only been friendly, walked to and from school with Arturo, and taken him to Ferris Center, where he was in the Church class of younger boys. Mrs. Alvarez was going to the Center, too, and sometimes she made the little meat pies that always reminded Pablo of Puerto Rico, and brought them to the Torres family. Then she and Mamita would have a good visit, talking about their homes in Puerto Rico and about New York, and how Arturo's dad had left them. But all that would not be interesting to Miss Lester.

"I just liked him, I guess. I knew how he felt those first days. I didn't do anything, really."

Miss Lester, smiling, shook her head as if she did not believe that was all there was to it.

As the days grew colder, Christmas drew nearer. Pablo was glad that Anita had accepted the North American Santa Claus to take the place of the visit of the Three Kings on January sixth.

"How could the camels get up to the third floor? Of course they can't. Santa Claus is better, anyway. All the girls are talking about him and I'm so excited!" This had laid Pablo's fears.

Ferris Center was bristling with activity immediately after Thanksgiving, in preparation for the long holiday. In his warm bed at night, Pablo thought often of Miss Thomas and of the holiday season at Hanson House. He wished he could spread his arms and fly out across the water. He'd come down out of the blue sky right into the patio of Hanson House. He'd land at Miss Thomas's office door beside the big red rose bush. No one would have time to warn her that he was coming. Wouldn't she be surprised? But what clothing would he wear? He'd have to have heavy winter things when he left New York and then summer things as soon as he landed. Now that was a real problem! He must write and tell Miss Thomas all about Mr. Pat and Mr. Everett and about his drum classes.

Extra practice filled spare hours, now. Pablo worked hard to make his part in the Christmas play as good as possible. The African scene opened with the drum call to the village people to bring them together for news. This was easy, just seven even beats repeated several times. But as the story of the Christ Child unfolded, there had to be a danger signal. This was a warning to Joseph that he was to take his little family into Egypt. Pablo had to play the danger call softly, way back in another room, yet loud enough to sound in the auditorium. This took a good deal of practice alone and with the cast. He and Mr. Pat worked hard on it.

"Never do anything representing life in any

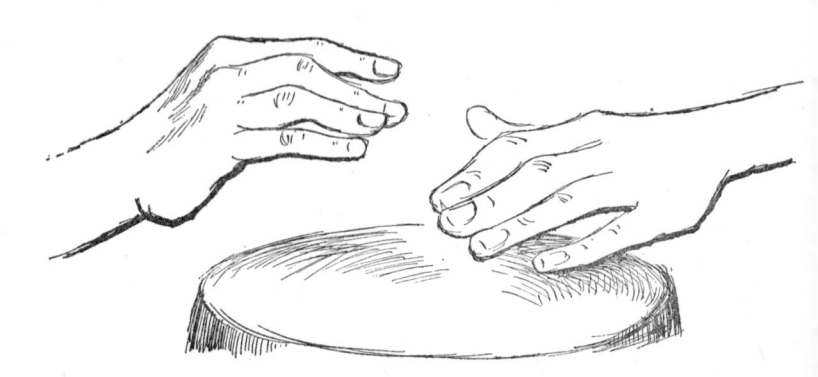

country unless you do it right," Mr. Pat said, and Pablo understood his friend's insistence on much practicing.

"Of course, there may be some people directly from Africa living around us here. But that is not the main reason for doing it right. Always do a job to the best of your power, Pablo, no matter what it is."

That is what has made Mr. Pat a wonderful musician, Pablo thought.

There were many other scenes for the play, from France and Syria, China and Brazil. The boys' Church School room became a jungle of costumes hanging on the hat hooks two weeks before the night of the performance. Arturo was one of the boys in the chorus and even Bingo was pressed into service with the other basketball boys to move scenery. Pablo was happy over the whole prospect. Even Josy was coming, Bingo said.

Mamita had made friends with Josefina after she learned that she worked in the same hotel with Don José. Why hadn't her husband told her about Josy being in the same place, Mamita asked one night at supper. He looked blank and then laughed.

"My dear, there are so many women working there, how should I notice her? I never see her around here so I would not know who she is."

"But she knew you, José, and that the others like you. Bingo told Pablo so."

Don José only shook his head and laughed and patted her hand. But Pablo was proud of him. Everyone liked strong, kind Don José. And now Josy was

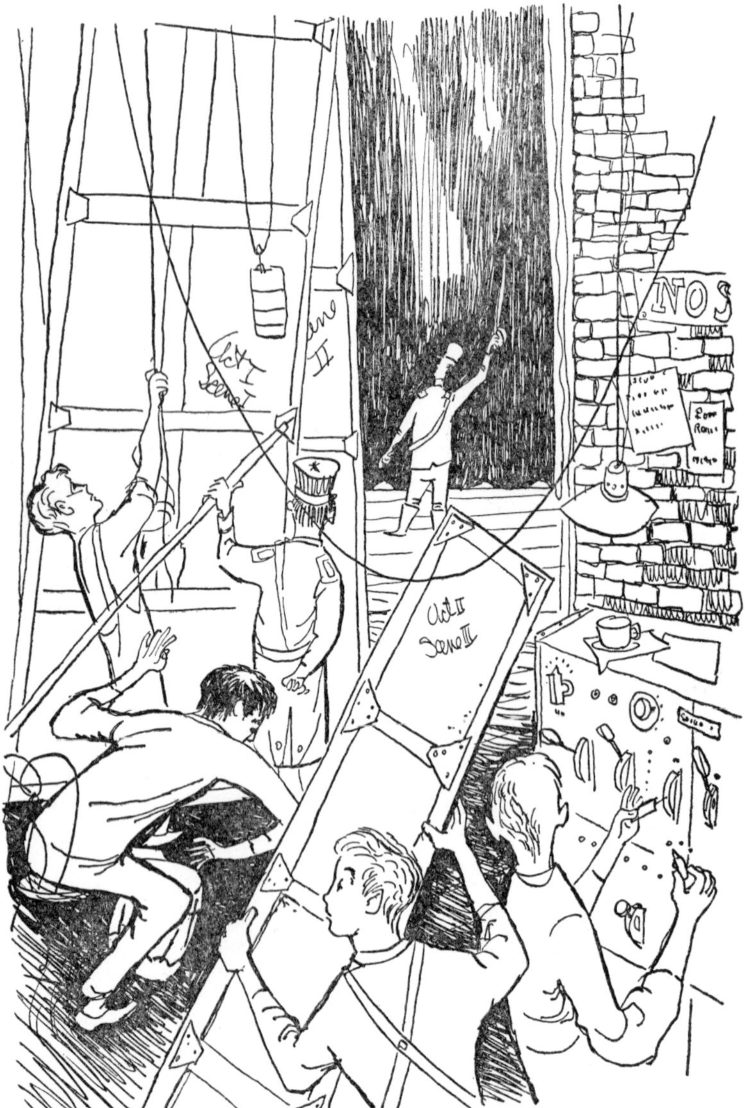
Act I Scene I
Scene II
Act II Scene III
NO S

being much kinder to Bingo since she had begun visiting with Mamita. That made Pablo feel a lot better when he left Bingo at the bottom of his flight of steps.

The Torres apartment was gay for Christmas. Anita brought home bright paper chains to hang from the swinging lamp cord to the corners of the doors and paper angels and snowflakes to paste on the glass of the windows. On the little table in the parlor stood a small tree that Papa had bought. Pablo spent two dollars for lights and colored balls and figures. What fun they all had trimming the tree the Sunday before Christmas.

Every few hours, Pablo went to take a peek at the gifts he had bought for the family, all wrapped and ready in his drawer.

"Ay, how good Christmas is, the birthday of our Christ," Grandmother kept saying, as she rocked back and forth in the old chair. Pablo knew she was crocheting something for Mamita, for she kept hiding her work when Mama came close to her.

The play and party afterward at Ferris Center were to be four days before Christmas and the day school vacations began. Pablo and Bingo spent the Saturday morning before in the office helping to wrap gifts and put on name tags, under the direction of Mr. Everett himself. Once Mr. Everett stopped behind Pablo and put his hand on his shoulder.

"Do you miss Puerto Rico very much, Pablo?" he asked.

"No, no, Mr. Everett, not too much. Everything

is good up here. I guess I'd like to see Miss Thomas and Hanson House, though. I wish she could come up here and see us!"

Mr. Everett gave his shoulder a squeeze and said, "Yes, so do I, Pablo," and then passed on to help Bingo with a bulky package for a kindergartener.

Pablo looked at the stack of gifts for the poor children and knew he had had a part in buying them. It was a mighty good feeling. Papa had always taught him to take out one-tenth of all the money he earned and give it to his church or to someone that needed it. And so, now, some of his paper route money was in that stack of gifts, and he was glad. He was glad Papa believed in giving a tenth, which he called "tithing." Miss Thomas used to say that tithing was the least people should give back to God's work.

The night of the play snow was falling over the city, soft and white and silent. Two other snows had fallen during November and Anita had nearly gone wild with joy. But this was by far the most beautiful.

As the Torres family, all except Grandmother, and Bingo and Josy walked toward Ferris Center, they heard Christmas music from radios along the street. Pablo wished they had a radio at home so they could hear music whenever they wished. Maybe, some day—

The play was a great success. Everyone said so. As Pablo was putting away his drum, Mr. Pat came into the room.

"Good work, Pablo. You did it just right. I'm

proud of you. And, by the way, you're ready to play in the orchestra now. I need another drummer."

That was all Pablo needed to make the night perfect. Or so he thought until he came across Mama and Mrs. Alvarez in a corner of the Center parlor, sitting close together on a sofa. Mamita had a letter in her hand. Could he believe his ears? She was reading! But Mamita could not read. She never had known how! He stood for a moment, listening. Mamita was so intent that she did not see him until she had finished two pages. Then she looked up and gave a start.

Pablo could only look at her. The expression on his face struck her funny for she began to laugh and, getting up, put her arm across his shoulder as if to comfort him.

"I did not mean for you to know until Christmas day, Pablito. Yes, I can read. You see, while you delivered papers, I came here for lessons three times a week."

She rustled the sheet she had been reading. "Mrs. Alvarez was not sure she understood all this letter from her husband. Now she does! He is really coming home to her and Arturo next month. Isn't that wonderful news?"

Pablo saw for the first time that Mrs. Alvarez was crying. Funny how women cry when they should be laughing, he thought. Why, even Mamita had tears in her eyes. It was time for him to leave. And he did with the wonderful knowledge singing to him: Mamita had learned to read!

As Don José walked home beside Pablo that night he put an envelope in the boy's hand.

"What is it?" Pablo asked.

"Maybe something for the new drum," **Papito** said. "Look at it."

As they passed under a street light, Pablo pulled a check from the envelope. It read, "Sixty-five dollars" and was signed by Pedro Quiñones.

"But this is yours, Papito. Don Pedro owed it to you."

"He did, son, but you used Mr. Pat's gift for the tickets, remember? No, this really belongs to you."

Sixty-five dollars. Why, he was rich. No other boy he knew had that much money. Think of the things he could buy with it, almost everything he wanted. A wonderful big new drum, and clothing, and a bicycle, and a basketball, and he could go to camp in the summer. His mind ran on and on and he could hardly keep from running with his feet, too.

When they entered the apartment they found Grandmother asleep in her chair by the kitchen window. She stirred and smiled when they called her, and when she was finally awake, explained, "I certainly was asleep, but not in bed. Oh my dears, how beautiful the Christmas music was, from across the way, through the window. I had to listen closely so I could hear it. Over the radio it came, all about the infant Jesus and the shepherds and the star. Just like the children always sing in Borinquen at Christmas time."

It was the first time Pablo had heard Grandmother use the original name of their island in many months.

Poor Grandmother. How he wished they had a radio in their apartment so she did not have to sit by a cold window to hear the music. He fingered the check in his pocket. Then he began to wonder. Why hadn't Papito kept the money and said nothing about it? The check was made out to him and Pablo knew that he had a struggle to pay the rent and get food for all of them. Then he remembered Mr. Ling's words, "and honest at all times." Papito should get a Good Citizenship Award himself for he was all that Mr. Ling said, and more.

Pablo kept wondering as he got ready for bed. Did the sixty-five dollars really belong to him? True, it replaced the gift Mr. Pat sent. But he began thinking of all the things his family needed to be comfortable in this cold weather. Mamita needed a jacket to go under her coat, and a new dress to wear to the Center. Anita did not have a snow suit like the other little girls for snowy days. Papa needed warmer shirts and his shoes were wearing out and he never wore gloves, even when the wind was piercing cold.

Sixty-five dollars minus the tenth that he would give Mr. Everett for really poor children. That left fifty-eight dollars and fifty cents. He lay in his narrow cot a long time before going to sleep, thinking about the check. Only two more days until Christmas. Only two more days and he had sixty-five dollars. I—am—rich! I—am—rich! His mind went around in circles until he thought he was Santa Claus flying across the moon, and in his sleigh he had gifts for all his family, friends, and Hanson House, for Ferris Center, and for everyone in all the world!

CHAPTER THIRTEEN

THE PICNIC

Winter seemed endless. Pablo wondered what summer and flowers and a warm sun and cotton shirts and pants would be like.

Ever since that night of the play last Christmas when he had received the check for sixty-five dollars, he had known that his family was comfortably warm, even in the coldest days. He had divided the money among the members of his family, keeping only enough for the big surprise on Christmas morning, a small table radio. As days began to grow warmer, now, Grandmother dozed by the radio hours on end with a smile on her face as Spanish music and Spanish talking made her content. When Pablo passed her she would often pat his arm and say, "My Pablito, my dear grandson."

But now it was May. Pablo awoke early this morning and bounced off his cot in great excitement.

Today, Don Romero's Church School class was going to Mr. Pat's farm in Westchester County, a long trip on the train. Best of all, each boy had been allowed to invite one guest. Bingo was going with Pablo. To Pablo's surprise, Miguel had asked Tap and he was going. It was not really strange, though, since they lived in the same apartment house. Now, however, as he got into his clothes, Pablo wondered what might happen because no one had asked Gus. But it did not worry him.

What a grand day for all the fun ahead! He breathed deeply of the warm sun-filled air as he and Bingo went to the Center. The crowd was already gathering. Don Romero checked his list as they arrived and finally called, "Off we go. Subway uptown."

The boys had been told not to bring money for their fare. All expenses would be cared for. By whom? Mr. Pat?

Don Romero bought subway tokens at the little booth at the foot of the steps and put one in the turnstile slot as each boy pushed his way through.

The ride to Grand Central Station was as rough as he remembered from last fall. But he did not mind for now he was a real New Yorker and not afraid any more.

When they came into the big station, the boys stayed close together, with Don Romero walking ahead of them. Many of the boys had not seen the station before, Pablo could tell from their questions, and so he listened and learned. They stood before the tremendous colored picture overhead across one end, a little girl and her mother in a field of bright flowers. Pablo felt as if the girl were going to speak to them and he wished that Anita could see it. Then he looked up at the great ceiling with its stars and figures and didn't realize that the rest were leaving him. He looked down just in time to see the last of the boys going down the stairs. He followed on the run. On the lower level, they followed another ramp to the train that was waiting along the platform in the half light.

Finally, the crowd from Ferris Center was settled for the trip. Though there was room for three on one side of the aisle and two on the other, they sat two and two. This was not the rush hour, Don Romero explained, so there was plenty of room. Miguel and Tap sat across the aisle from Pablo and Bingo.

Now they were pulling out and it seemed a long time to Pablo before they came out into sunlight again. When they did, they were on a high bridge over the street and passing streets that ran under the tracks.

"Have you never been out here before, Pablo?" Don Romero asked, sitting down beside him.

"No, I've never even been on a train before," Pablo answered.

"That's Harlem down there, Pablo," Don Romero went on explaining. "This is probably the poorest part of New York City. Thousands of people live within a few blocks and many families in even one room, sometimes. You should be very glad Don José did not have to bring you here to live when

THE PICNIC

you came. Lots and lots of Puerto Ricans have to settle here because they cannot find anywhere else."

Pablo looked down on five boys playing with a ball in a dirty square back of a tall building. Streets were filled with people and papers and garbage cans and pushcarts of fruits and vegetables for sale. The streets seemed much narrower and dirtier than in his part of the city. Women sat on their steps visiting and Pablo wondered if they were speaking Spanish.

"But now you see these fine apartment houses. Blocks of such houses as we just passed were torn down by the city to make place for these. The same people can rent these if they will keep their places clean and in repair," Don Romero was saying.

"Is there a Ferris Center here?" Pablo asked.

"Not exactly the same, Pablo. But there are missions that are doing wonderful things for Harlem. One of them was started by some young students from one of the seminaries in the city. Maybe some day you would like to visit one of them with me."

Before long, they were passing through town after town and Pablo caught a glimpse of bright gardens and big white houses and a swimming pool under queer drooping trees. He wondered what Mr. Pat's place would be like. Only one thing marred Pablo's complete happiness. He heard Tap talking across the aisle to Miguel about Gus, evidently bragging about what wonderful things he dared to do. Why couldn't he forget Gus for today and just be one of the Ferris Center fellows?

"Next stop is ours, boys. Out this way," and Don

Romero led the way down steps when the train stopped. A smiling trainman stood beside Mr. Pat on the platform while the crowd tumbled to the platform beside him.

"No broken necks, I hope, Mr. Patterson," he said as he swung up the steps as the train pulled off.

"Everyone here?" Mr. Pat called over the heads and a volley of "yes's" reassured him. "This way then to my station wagon." They piled into a big car with the name "Old Orchard Farm" on the outside.

"What's an orchard?" Pablo asked. Bingo stuck out his chest. "Orchard? Why, it's a lot of pink trees. We got a picture of one." Pablo remembered the picture over Josy's sink.

"Partly right, Bingo," Mr. Patterson said over his shoulder, "but it's flowers that are pink. Sometimes they're white, if the tree is pear, for instance. When the blossoms fall off, the fruit comes. We have apples and pears and peaches in our orchard."

As they came up the driveway, Pablo could hardly believe his eyes. A big house seemed to go on and on, with a great big glass window in the front. At one end was a screened porch and through the porch he could see the orchard, a mass of bloom.

"Boys, I want you to know Mrs. Patterson," Mr. Pat said, simply, and Pablo found his hand being shaken. He looked up into friendly blue eyes that made him feel comfortable right away. They reminded him of Miss Thomas.

"We're so glad you have come," she said.

THE PICNIC 127

The boys were shown the entire house, from playroom for winter, in the basement, to the library on the second floor and then the laundry and even the storeroom on the first floor.

"I have a small orchestra out here, too, among our neighbors," Mr. Pat explained, "and we keep a few of the instruments in here." Pablo saw a very large drum standing on a table in one corner and wondered how it would sound.

They were soon called to dinner out on the back lawn under a huge tree. Juicy steaks were sizzling over a charcoal fire.

"We are so lucky to be able to get charcoal for our fire out here," Mrs. Pat said to Don Romero, as she turned the steaks. Pablo had not seen any charcoal since they left Puerto Rico. He would not tell her that Mama always cooked over charcoal in their little lean-to kitchen down in the island. She would just think it funny and perhaps laugh. She would not understand how good the charcoal smoke smelled when a boy woke in the morning and knew Mamita was getting breakfast. He'd stand on this side of the fire just a moment and smell the smoke. No one would know what he was doing so he would not have to explain.

At last they were told to come and get it. Steak between slices of white bread with any sauce they wanted, and fried potatoes, mountains of them, and big red tomatoes. Then came chocolate sundaes and even Pablo had trouble finding room for everything. There was much laughing and teasing and the extra boys who had been invited seemed as much at home as those from Don Romero's class.

Pablo wished that the day could go on and on. How many hours were left? Don Romero seemed to sense his question for he just then made an announcement.

"We have until five o'clock, boys, about three hours. Mr. Pat says you may do anything you like until we have to leave. There's a volleyball court on the north side, and pingpong on the porch. You can go to see the animals in the barn. A farmer is out there to tell you about things."

"Can we climb?" Bingo asked.

"Do you mean in the trees?" Mr. Pat asked.

Bingo nodded. "I guess so, if you are careful," Mr. Pat answered, adding, "only not in the fruit trees, please. We want those blossoms to make fruit and not be knocked off before they have a chance."

The boys scattered. "Me for volleyball," Bingo shouted and was off for the court. Pablo decided to walk toward the barn and Miguel joined him.

"Where's Tap?" Pablo asked.

THE PICNIC

"Gone with Bingo to play volleyball," Miguel answered.

Pablo had never in his life seen so many chickens and cows and pigs and to think that they all belonged to one family. The farmer explained to them how many eggs he gathered a day, and how much milk the cows gave. He took them to see the supplies of feed and answered patiently the scores of questions. Then he showed the "milking parlor," as he called it, where cows were milked and the milk put in cans and chilled immediately before being sent out on trucks. When they had at last seen everything in the barn, they thanked the farmer and walked on toward the orchard.

"Mr. Pat must be very rich," Pablo said.

"Yeah, I guess so. Mrs. Pat is a painter, you know, the kind that sells pictures for lots of money, so that helps, too, I imagine. There she is now, under that big tree," Miguel added.

Mrs. Patterson stood before a big picture that had been placed on a three-legged rack, and she was painting. A blanket was spread on the ground under her feet and on it lay a wooden case of paints and rags.

She looked up and smiled. "Like painting?" she asked. "Come on. Don't mind walking on the blanket. I keep it because this ground is wet from last night's rain. I'll show you what I'm doing if you stand back of me."

Pablo thought he had never seen anything so beautiful. A branch of the tree in full bloom lay across the top of the picture, with a part of the dark trunk along the left side. In the distance stood the house, with the porch and blue awning and flower beds. Both boys stood fascinated as she worked on, putting a touch of deeper green here, a bit of yellow in the sunlight, more blue in the sky, picking out one color after another from the board she held with her thumb.

Pablo was just thinking how very quiet it was when, from overhead, a tearing sound made them jump. Crack! Crack! The boys ran from under the tree. Mrs. Pat picked up her picture and was right behind them. When they looked back into the branches, there were Bingo and Tap. Tap was on a lower limb, crawling down as fast as he could come. But above him, Bingo was far out on an old branch that was fast breaking away from the trunk. His face was pale with fear as he grasped at one branch after another trying to swing onto something safe before his limb fell with him. Pablo remembered once looking up at another person against the sky.

"Quick! The blanket," he yelled, just as Tap reached the ground. Pablo gave the blanket a yank that sent the painting box flying. The others got the idea and each grabbed a corner.

"Pull it hard!" Pablo yelled again, leaning back with all his strength, holding the blanket chest-high. Tap and Miguel and Mrs. Pat did the same just as the branch gave way and Bingo fell crashing through the tree. He lit on the improvised net, a bundle of boy, with no life apparently in him. His fall had been broken and Pablo felt sure he did not hit the ground. They laid the blanket and boy gently down. Mrs. Pat knelt beside him.

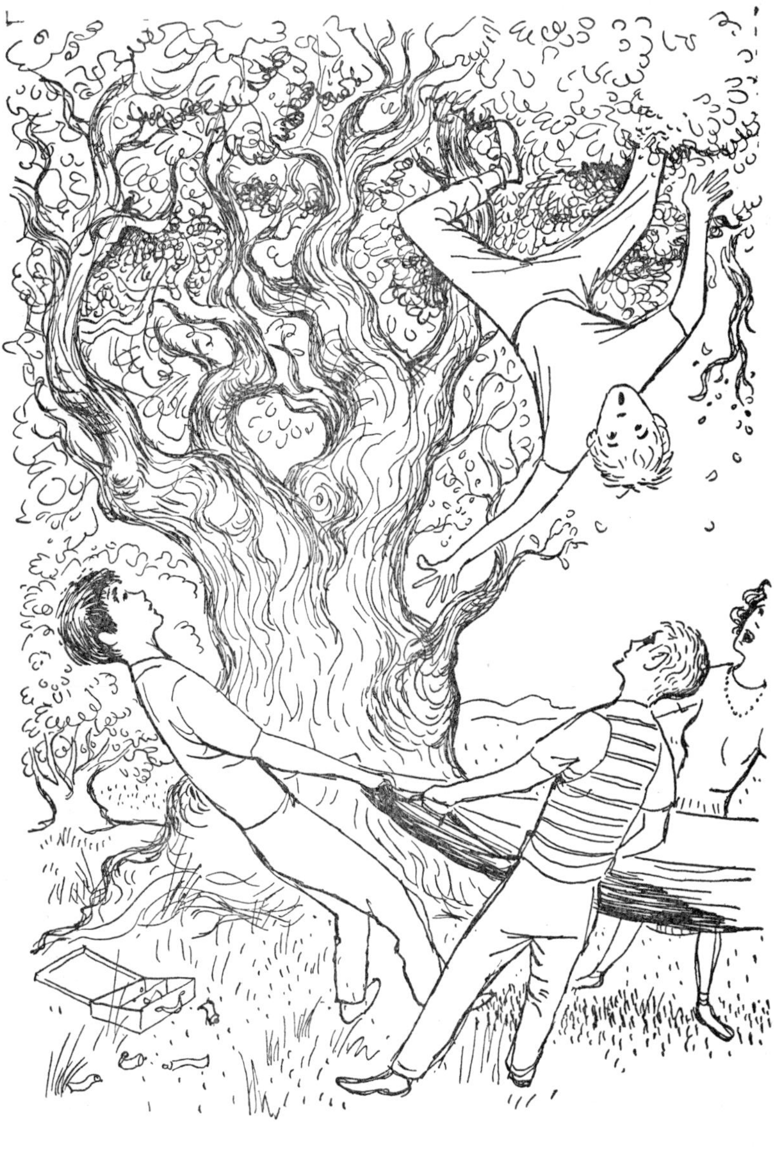

"Mr. Pat? Where is he?" Pablo asked.

"He's not here!" Mrs. Pat's voice sounded very unsteady. "He's with Don Romero and the car at the next farm, two miles away. He should not have left us this way. He said he would be right back."

"Can we telephone?" Miguel asked.

"No, the phone's been out of order for two days. But we must get help. He isn't coming to." Bingo lay white and still on the blanket.

Then Pablo remembered. "I'll get him," he called as he began running straight for the storeroom. He grabbed the big drum from the corner and then, out on the lawn, he began to beat the drum with all his strength: one, two, three, four, five, six, seven,—one, two, three—and then twice he repeated the call. With every ounce of arm strength he then sounded the danger signal, over and over, the signal of the African tribes. Of course the boys had come running, thinking he had gone crazy or was playing a game that looked very silly. He paid no attention. He must get Mr. Pat.

After what seemed an eternity, he saw the station wagon tearing down the road and heard the answering auto horn blowing all the way. The car swung into the drive and only then did Pablo stop and drop the drum to the ground. He had trouble in not following it himself, he felt so limp.

But he got into the car and led the men to the orchard, explaining in short words what had happened. Not until they got there did Pablo begin to wonder who the third man was. He was the one now kneeling beside Bingo.

"Nothing serious. He's coming out of it," the man said, after examining Bingo. "He hit his head, evidently, in the fall and fainted," and he got to his feet. "Say, why isn't he hurt worse if that's where he fell from?" he said, looking up at the hanging limb.

Mrs. Pat explained. Pablo felt embarrassed as her story went on. Anyone could have thought of the blanket and drum. He just happened to be there to do it, that was all.

"I saw firemen use a net once," he explained. "It wasn't anything, really."

The boys had gone back to their games, Miguel and Tap with them. Pablo helped Mrs. Pat gather up the contents of her painting case. Mr. Pat and Don Romero were sitting beside Bingo, who was propped on pillows by this time.

"Young fellow, it's a good thing you thought of that drum. A few more minutes of this fright and I think we might have had Mrs. Pat as a real patient," Mr. Pat said. "We were in Dr. Jackson's garden looking at his roses when I began to hear something strange from this direction. As soon as I heard the danger signal, we came in a hurry."

"How's the patient feeling?" Dr. Jackson asked, and Bingo answered, "I'm okay, I guess," and got unsteadily to his feet.

Before long, Mrs. Pat called the boys for more ice cream on the porch before they had to leave. Bingo had nothing to say as he and Pablo walked slowly to the house. It was not until they were on the train that he talked.

"I could have been dead by now, if it hadn't been for you," he said.

Pablo had nothing he could think of to say and so went on looking out the window.

"We thought it'd be fun to climb that there big old fruit tree, even though Mr. Pat said not in fruit trees. It had plenty of flowers to spare a few and we thought we would not be seen. We were just up there when Mrs. Pat came out and began to paint. Then we couldn't get down."

"I thought you were going to play volleyball," Pablo said.

"We did go over but the fellows didn't seem to want us very much so we went on out there. I got so numb trying to sit still so as not to be heard that I couldn't hold to nothin' when that branch began to go. You were swell to pull the blanket, and all."

Pablo knew it was Bingo's way of thanking him so it was all right. Pretty soon the boy beside him was fast asleep and Pablo was glad.

Miguel leaned over once and whispered, "Tap says he thinks you're all right," and Pablo grinned his thanks for the compliment.

What a day it had been! Pablo was mighty glad when he and Bingo climbed their apartment stairs and he could let the other boy go on to his home and Josefina. He was more glad than he could remember to be back with his own family in their own apartment, as he opened the door and closed it behind him.

CHAPTER FOURTEEN

GRADUATION

Pablo did not say anything about the exciting experience at Old Orchard Farm. It was only through Don Romero that Don José brought the news home. Each member took the story in his own way. Grandmother repeated, "My Pablo," more often than usual. Mama wept a little. Anita told him how many of her little friends hoped he would be their boy friend when they got older. Don José just let him know that he was proud of him. Pablo only hoped everyone would soon forget all about it. As for Bingo, he seemed happy playing in the Ferris Center gym and still delivered papers for Pablo on Tuesdays.

But there was trouble between Gus and Tap. Gus would not speak to Tap since the trip. Pablo sensed trouble brewing between them from the angry looks and silence of Gus whenever Tap was around. Miguel was worried, too, and wondered if he'd done the right thing to ask Tap for the picnic.

"Sure you did all right, Miguel. They'll have to settle it between them. Gus could have been invited by someone if he'd quit being such a smart bully to everyone."

How soon they'd settle it Pablo had little idea when he talked with Miguel that afternoon at recess. He wasn't ready nor expecting the fight he found going on in the school washroom that very afternoon after three-thirty. Mrs. Henry had needed his help in straightening the room, since the janitor was sick. He was on his way out when he ran into the fight. He didn't know what to do. They were going at it hard and heavy. First one was on top, then the other, as they rolled and punched on the floor. Gus must have suddenly realized that Pablo was standing by, for he broke away from Tap and before Pablo realized what was happening, came at him like a mad boy.

"You, too, you bum," he said between closed teeth and gave Pablo a hard blow on the chest that nearly floored him. Pablo's right arm came up in a well-directed blow under Gus's chin that sent him flying backward and down. Pablo was on top of him in a flash, pinning his wrists to the cement. Pablo didn't like to fight, but he could if it was necessary and this was one of the times.

Gus struggled to get free and then gave up. Pablo brushed off his suit and, without a word, walked out of the building. He supposed the others followed. He did not look back.

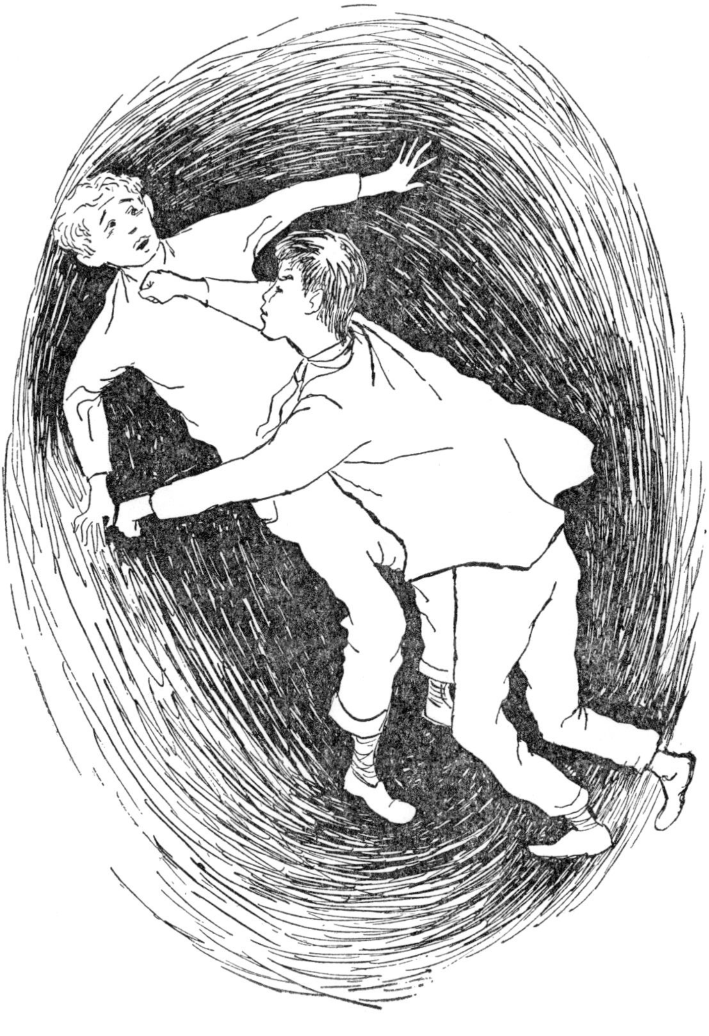

No mention was made of that fight. The following Friday night, however, Pablo was not surprised to see both Tap and Gus at the gym at Ferris Center and was glad that the other fellows seemed to be accepting them. At least, they were not being mean and the two newcomers were happy in the far end of the gym with one of the balls.

Before Pablo could change his shoes for a real basketball workout, Mr. Everett called him into his office.

"I have a surprise for you, Pablo," Mr. Everett began, smiling at him from behind his desk. "There won't be any basketball next Friday, for I want all of you to come to my wedding in the auditorium."

Mr. Everett getting married? Pablo had never thought much about Mr. Everett not being married. He guessed he should be glad since Mr. Everett looked so very happy.

"We have something we want you to do, Pablo. Will you light the candles on the altar just before the wedding march? We'll have a robe for you so you need not worry about clothes."

Of course, he'd be glad to do anything Mr. Everett wanted. Pablo wondered on the way home who the bride was, but since he did not know Mr. Everett's friends, he would not know her even if he had asked. There was to be a rehearsal in the church at Ferris Center on Tuesday at five o'clock. He wished he could tell the family, but Mr. Everett had sworn him to secrecy.

"We don't want it told until an invitation for

everyone is put on the bulletin board next Wednesday," he had said.

By the time Tuesday came, Pablo had grown curious. Why all this secrecy? When he told Mr. Pat that he would not be at orchestra practice, he asked no questions and did not seem surprised.

"Come to my office before rehearsal," Mr. Everett had said. Pablo stood now in front of the office door and knocked.

"Come in," Mr. Everett answered and Pablo pushed the door open. A lady was sitting in front of the desk with her back to the door.

"I'm glad you're here, Pablo." Mr. Everett was smiling. "Come and meet my childhood sweetheart and the future Mrs. Everett."

Pablo wished this part of it were over. He didn't like to meet strangers. Let's get on to the rehearsal, he was thinking as he came around the chair and the lady rose. The next thing Pablo knew, arms were around him and someone was both laughing and crying.

"Pablo! My, but it is good to see you!"

Pablo drew back to make sure he was not dreaming.

"Why, Miss Thomas. It's really you?"

"Who's crying for what?" Mr. Everett finally said, his arms around them both. "Break this up. We have work to do," he said, laughing.

"You didn't guess, did you, Pablo?" Miss Thomas asked.

He shook his head. Of course he hadn't.

"You didn't know that we were sweethearts long ago, and that her letter to me about you started our writing again last winter," Mr. Everett explained.

"And here I am to stay, Pablo. I got here this morning from Hanson House, flying up last night," Miss Thomas added.

"What will happen to Hanson House, Miss Thomas?" Pablo asked.

"I've been training Senorita Margarita and she is in charge now. Hanson House is in good hands. Mine are needed here beside this man's," and she took Mr. Everett's hand affectionately.

The Torres family had never seen a North American wedding. Even Grandmother, dressed in her best, came in the taxi that Mr. Everett sent for her and Mamita. The hall was a garden of flowers. Don Antonio beamed at Pablo as he came from lighting the candles. He had told Pablo he would lend the tall palm trees in tubs, without charge, and when Pablo told Mr. Everett, Don Antonio had gotten the orders for all the wedding flowers. The man from Aguadilla outdid himself in furnishing the very best.

There was the rice-throwing as the young couple got into their car to drive off. Grandmother thought this a great waste of good rice.

"It's custom, Mama. You know we have our customs in Puerto Rico, too. They marry only once," Mamita explained and Grandmother was satisfied.

School was nearly over now. One more week of the school year. Then Pablo was to spend the summer helping Mr. Fitzman in the store. He was almost envious of Anita and her chance to go to a camp for two weeks. How he'd love to be in a boys' camp. Maybe, some day. How often he had said that during the year and many of his dreams had come true.

In the bedroom closet hung Pablo's new suit, the gift of his family for his graduation. Daily practices for graduation were held in the assembly hall at school, until Pablo thought the class would certainly do everything on Friday night perfectly.

The farewell assembly was to be Thursday morning. Parents of graduates were invited. Don José managed to have the half day off since he could not be there for graduation and he had never been in Pablo's school.

Pablo was now showing him about the building with much pride. Then they heard the orchestra begin to play and Pablo said it was time to join Mamita in the graduates' section. Not many fathers were there and Pablo was glad Papito cared enough to come. He was sorry for the fellows whose dads never came to school.

The first part of the program was much like all assemblies, with orchestra music and singing. Miss Lester made final announcements about graduation, and greeted the parents.

"And now, pupils and friends of this school, we have come to the announcement I am sure you have been waiting for."

The Good Citizenship Award, of course. Pablo

had not thought much about it for a long time. But it would be interesting to see who did get it and he or she would be a lucky person.

Silence fell on the auditorium. Feet stopped scraping. Whispering died away.

"I am going to call on our good friend, Mr. Wu Ling, to present this award," Miss Lester was saying. Mr. Ling smiled and bowed while the people clapped.

"My fellow citizens," he began and Pablo remembered the first time he had addressed them last winter, "many years ago I came from China to this big city, as I have told you before. I came to this school and have learned what it means to be a good citizen of this America. It is a great honor this morning, as chairman of the selecting committee, to give this award to one who has this year shown that he has learned the lesson that never changes, no matter how old we grow. I am going to ask Pablo Torres to come to the platform."

Clapping! Laughing around him! Someone lifting him by the elbows, Papa and Mamita on each side. He was walking blindly toward the platform.

"Pablo," Mr. Ling began, "we're not going to embarrass you by telling of all you have done for this school, of the things the committee knows of that proved your good citizenship. We know of your kindness to friends, to a sick child in my apartment house, how you were honest when it would have been easier to be dishonest, how you saved a fellow pupil from a bad accident. Your teachers and fellow pupils give you this award with their pride in you and love and best wishes for you as you go on into high school. May God bless you and your family and all boys and girls like you who will continue to make America great."

A representative from the Board of Education then gave him a medal in a leather case, and the next few minutes were an eternity. Congratulations, handshaking, pats on the back, Mamita crying, Anita dancing around him, Papito accepting congratulations, too.

At last they were in the street. But the day was not over. Mr. Pat stood at the door of his car and motioned Pablo to enter. Right there on the front seat were Anita and Grandmother.

What was that on the seat in front of him? "It's from Ferris Center, Pablo. Long may you beat that drum, my boy," Mr. Pat said, "and now take it on your lap and make room for your parents. We're going to Old Orchard Farm to celebrate. Look behind you."

Through the back window, Pablo saw Mr. and

Mrs. Everett in their car, waving to him, and Don Romero and Bingo were in the back seat.

"They came back from their honeymoon a day early to help with this great day," Mr. Pat went on. "We knew what was coming because Miss Lester had told Don Romero. Off we go, now, or else Mrs. Pat will say I spoiled the turkey dinner that's waiting for us. By the way, do you like turkey, Pablo?"

Pablo could only nod his head. He was too happy to speak.